Hunting Werewolves and Other Bad Dates

THE GRIMM BROTHERHOOD
BOOK ONE

KEL CARPENTER

WITH
MEG ANNE

To Hostess cupcakes ... may you never be squished.

And then everyone was dead.

Jacob Grimm, *The Brothers Grimm: The Complete Fairy Tales*

Hostess Cupcakes

My speedometer inched near one hundred twenty. I let out a low whistle under my breath as I beat my hands against the steering wheel like drums, Duran Duran drowning out my thoughts.

The faded sign welcoming me to Farrow's Square shrunk to the size of a pinprick in my rearview mirror. I whipped around a sharp curve with a quick stomp on the brakes and screech of my wheels. The sign disappeared entirely.

Singing at the top of my lungs, a murder of crows scattered before me. I flipped them the bird as I floored it toward town. The Appalachian Mountains and roadkill were all I'd seen for the past few hours as I hightailed it back to the place I swore I'd never return to.

I should have known better.

Never say never.

It's a great way to tempt fate.

And mine? She was a bitch.

My right hand slipped from the wheel as I reached to

my passenger seat, patting it until I found my purse. My eyes flicked between the road and the tattered multicolor monstrosity my best friend bought me for my eighteenth birthday four years ago.

My hand latched onto something smooth. I pulled it out.

Mascara.

"Ugh," I groaned under my breath as I tossed it in the back. Trying again, I pushed the crap aside, rummaging with half my attention until I felt the crinkle of smooth plastic.

"Yes," I purred, pulling it out.

The golden wrapper of a condom was *not* what I was looking for.

"Motherfucker," I muttered, tossing that in the back too.

Third time's a charm. Isn't that what everyone says? I rolled with it, cruising down the highway and going straight past the little town I'd grown up in. My house was still a half-hour out and the thick rain clouds overhead didn't encourage me to stop when I had the top down on my convertible BMW.

Resigned to carrying on, I reached for the purse again, feeling around for the pack of Hostess cupcakes I know I put in there. My hands just found purchase when something ran into the road.

Large and furry. It skidded across my periphery, coming to stop in my lane.

I dropped the cupcakes and slammed on the brakes. My hands moved on the wheel, trying to dodge, but it was too late.

The last thing I saw before the car flipped were red eyes staring straight at me.

I didn't even have time to scream as my car went airborne. It careened to the side; the wheels unable to hold their grip any longer.

My brain rattled, and my heart squeezed as the world turned over.

Something crunched. Pain erupted everywhere. Stars exploded behind my eyes.

And then, it all went black.

All for some fucking Hostess cupcakes.

WHEN MY EYES OPENED, I was not a Salem pancake as I'd expected. Not a crazy assumption given the open convertible doing somersaults down the highway. You know, that and the pain. I wasn't even on the road anymore.

Blinking a few times, I looked around at the scattered trees and clear night sky. I was standing in some kind of forest.

"The fuck?" I asked, craning my neck as I tried to figure out where I was, let alone how I'd gotten there.

"You can't stay here," a voice whispered behind me.

I jumped and spun; arms already lifted to defend myself when I faltered. The girl was about twelve with an old-timey grace that felt way too out of place for Farrow's Square. Her hair was a dark curtain that hung down her back, her dress some kind of antique black lace that covered her from neck to ankle. And she was pale, with black eyes that were far too old for her young face.

There was no way I was going to let some kid from the Addams family know she'd just scared the ever-living crap out of me.

"Listen, Morticia, you don't just sneak up on people in the middle of the woods. That's a good way to go and get yourself killed."

She blinked, a smile tilting up her lips. It was the creepiest fucking thing I'd ever seen. "That's not my name."

I scowled at her, anger swiftly replacing my fear. "Like I give two shits, kid."

"You need to go back."

"Back where?"

She lifted a hand, pointing in the direction of poor Bassy; my car was a mess of smoke and flame. "It's not safe for you to stay here."

"And you think a pile of burning metal is safer?"

She didn't move, her body inhumanly still as she stared at me. "It's not time for you to walk the in-between," she tried again when I still hadn't taken a step in the direction she pointed. "If you don't go back, someone else will claim what you have abandoned."

"What the fuck are you talking about?" A normal person might have phrased that differently, but these days I had three modes: angry Salem, hungry Salem, and super angry Salem. Nowhere in there was there room for a filter.

Not-Morticia scowled at me, taking two steps forward to shove me in the direction of the crumpled mess that used to be my car. "Go. Now!"

I felt like someone had dumped a bucket of ice water

over me. I gasped, struggling to catch my breath as my mind was suddenly filled with memories that weren't mine. Before I had time to process anything, she pointed at something that lay prone beside the car.

Not something. Someone.

A body.

My body.

There was no missing the bubblegum pink hair matted with blood.

"You need to go back," Not-Morticia hissed. "They're coming."

Had I been looking at anything other than what could only be called my corpse, I might have thought to ask her who was coming, but instead, I started walking toward my body, drawn to it like a magnet.

Soon I was on my knees, looking up at the girl like she could tell me how it were possible that I was both dead and yet alive.

"Go back," she said again, her voice so much older than her face. "Your answers wait for you on the other side."

Not knowing what else to do, I lifted my hand and rested it on top of my shoulder.

My chest constricted, and I gasped. My eyes flew open, and I was no longer staring down at myself, but up at the sky.

Deep breaths, I thought to myself as I started to hyperventilate.

I was dead. I was so dead. Then I wasn't.

I looked down at my body. Scratches tore through my clothes. Dried blood made the material cling to me uncomfortably. I peeled my shirt up, trying to get a look at the damage. Despite the amount of blood and dirt stuck to me, my skin was smooth and even.

I let out a shaky breath.

Was I hallucinating?

I looked sideways at my car. My beautiful fucking car that was now totaled.

Nope. I was not hallucinating.

Slowly I moved to my feet, running through my options.

I could call my aunt, assuming I could find my phone, and maybe she could come pick me up. The only problem with that was that I looked like a dead person because I had been—and now I wasn't.

Weird things did happen all the time, though. Miracles. They just didn't usually happen to my family.

I scratched my head, and my stomach chose that moment to rumble. I put a hand to it, thinking back on those Hostess cupcakes. They sounded really good right now, and I'd definitely missed dinner.

I took a few slow steps toward the wreckage. Both sides of my car were slammed inwards. If not for the lack of a top it wouldn't be accessible at all. However, if I climbed carefully over the sharp, jagged sides, there was a chance I would be able to rummage around to see if the cupcakes were still there.

I patted my pockets to see if my phone was on me so I could use the flashlight.

Being hungry and newly-not-dead called for desperate measures.

Like eating before I decided how I planned to explain this.

Luckily for me, my phone was still in my pocket. I pressed my thumb down to open it. The lack of signal had me unsure whether this was a good or bad thing. Either way, the flashlight worked.

Cupcakes, here I come.

I was just starting to maneuver over the edge of the wreckage when a voice behind me said, "What the hell are you doing?"

A squeak left me as I jumped, falling sideways into the decrepit remainder of my car. I grunted, sitting up. Intense fluorescent light shined right in my face. I swatted it away, and the flashlight went flying.

Without the blinding brightness, I could see clearly again. The stranger in front of me was quite a looker. Dark hair. High cheekbones and a strong jaw. Stubble and full lips. I blinked twice, questioning for a moment if it were somehow possible I was still dead.

Then the blue eyes hardened.

Definitely not dead, I decided again.

"Who the fuck are you?" I demanded, pulling myself to my feet.

"How about we start with what the fuck you're doing trying to climb into a car that is on fire?" he snapped back.

My spine straightened, and my eyes narrowed. This guy might be hot, but I was not in the mood. Dying had a way of doing that to a girl. Besides, no one talked to me that way. I was Salem Fucking Kaine. My family practically owned this town.

Before I could fire off my own vitriol-fueled reply, his eyes flared wide and he looked me up and down. "Wait . . . were you in there?"

Remembering the blood, I faltered. Lying wasn't really my specialty, and with the way I looked right now, there really was no getting around it.

"Yup," I said, popping the p. Fuck it. It was the truth, after all.

He blinked, glancing between me and the car like he could come up with a rational explanation for how I was still breathing. Finally, he lifted his icy eyes back to my face. His pupils flared, and his expression softened, just for a second. "Salem?"

My jaw went slack, and I started to take a step back before I caught myself. I definitely didn't know this guy, and I hadn't lived here for over four years. There was no reason he should know my name. Crossing my arms, I cocked a hip and stared up at him, silently demanding an explanation. I wasn't stupid enough to give him more information without gathering some of my own.

"You're Shep's sister," he said, his expression hardened once more. "You already missed the funeral. Why come back now?"

And there it was. The reason I was back in this shithole. Okay, it wasn't a shithole. Not even close. But I hated it all the same. Ever since I'd crossed the state line into North Carolina, I'd practically choked on the memories that had consumed me. Each one crystalizing my anger and fueling my rage. *Damnit, Shep. I fucking told you this would happen.*

"I don't think that's any of your business," I said.

He glared at me. "Don't be too sure about that. I mean, I was there, and you weren't, so—"

"Finish that sentence. I dare you." The guy had a good six inches on me, maybe more. And his bicep was about the size of my thigh. Didn't mean I would hesitate to kick him straight in the dick. He might be bigger than me, but a good nut shot was the world's best equalizer.

A muscle ticked in his jaw. He looked about as angry as I felt, but the anger wasn't directed at me. He let out a sharp exhale and glanced away, staring hard at my car.

"Do you need a ride?"

"Uh . . ." I let out a shallow laugh. "I'm not about to get in a strange dude's car."

"I'm hardly a stranger, Salem. Shepard was my best friend." He said it like it should mean something to me.

I blinked at him. What did he want? A medal? Or maybe a cookie . . . I got a little distracted at the thought of cookies, my growling stomach taking that moment to make itself known.

"I might have a bag of M&M's in my car . . ." he said slowly.

I narrowed my eyes. "Really? Like that makes it any better?" I asked incredulously. "You're literally the fucking candy man—"

"Yeah, well, you totaled your car and you look dead on your feet. I can hear your stomach rumbling. Shepard said you were really into anything chocolate. Since you want to be a brat about this, I figured I could—"

"What?" I threw both hands up. "Lure me away with candy? Hmm? Did it ever occur to you that I might be waiting on someone?" I asked, crossing my arms over my chest once more.

"In the woods? By yourself? While you're doing god knows what in the car..." He lifted an eyebrow, giving me a condescending look.

I growled under my breath. Of all the people to come across me on my first hour back, it had to be this dickwad.

This was exactly what I meant about my family and miracles. Blessings didn't come without a curse. It looked like my way out of here was sexy as all get out and apparently knew my brother. Then he opened his mouth, and all I could think about were better ways to put it to use.

I ran a hand through my hair, already having forgotten the dried blood that made it stick together. My fingers snagged, and I cursed under my breath.

"Look," he said, letting out a sigh. "You've clearly had a rough night. I can just give you a ride back to your aunt's if you want. It's gotta be better than waiting out here all night until some rando trucker drives through and *maybe* gives you a ride back to town where you have enough service to actually make a call." He lifted both hands in surrender and inclined his head.

I pressed my lips together, debating it.

Unfortunately for me, he wasn't wrong.

"Fine," I said, moving away from what was left of my car. My black combat boots touched the forest floor and a pop from plastic exploding followed by a squish made my heart sink. Lifting my foot, I looked down where I'd just stepped.

Two smushed Hostess cupcakes spilled out of their crappy plastic wrapping.

"Ugh," I growled under my breath, my fists clenching as I realized what I'd done.

Stranger Danger beside me cocked his head. "You're pissed about stepping on shitty processed junk food more than your car? Or, I don't know—the injuries you likely have?"

"Shelve the judgment, dude. I can't control my totaled car. That ship has sailed. I can't change that I look like I was in a car accident and thrown from the fucking car." His eyes flashed with something, but I ignored it. "I can't even control the fact that I'm hungry because I missed dinner. Or how shit my life is right now. All I could control was finding and eating those fucking cupcakes until I figured out what I was going to do." I was shouting at a guy who looked like a god and that I did not know in the slightest, but I was at my wit's end tonight. "And apparently—I can't even fucking do that!"

He studied me, and it felt like his eyes could see straight through me. I couldn't recall a time I ever felt more exposed. "Come on; I think I have a jacket you can borrow in the car."

Something in his tone took away the fight in me. I was tired, and I really didn't have a better choice.

"Okay," I grumbled. "But there better be some M&M's."

He smirked.

"Don't even think about getting handsy," I warned him, giving him the side-eye. Not that I would mind. The guy looked like he knew what to do with his hands. I just felt better saying it.

He actually laughed at me. "In your dreams, Salem Kaine."

Stranger Danger

He held open the passenger door to his baby blue '79 Corvette convertible. I didn't know shit about what was under the hoods, but my twin had been obsessed with American muscle cars, so I'd picked up some knowledge from him. I certainly knew enough to recognize this one was in pristine condition.

"Huh, who knew you had manners?" I snarked, sliding into the seat.

He shut the door and moved around the front of the car to the driver's side. "That mouth of yours is going to get you in trouble."

I snorted. "It already does. Daily."

He shook his head. "Why am I not surprised?" He climbed in and the engine roared to life. He twisted the knob on the radio, muting the deafening sound of The Smiths as he pulled away from the side of the road and took off.

I could stand the silence for all of thirty seconds before blurting, "So are you going to tell me your name, or should

I just keep referring to you in my head as Stranger Danger?"

"I thought for sure the chocolate would be your first priority. Glove box, by the way," he said. I was already reaching, pulling out the bag of candy and ripping it open as he finally answered my question. "Which name do you want? I have three of them."

The way he said it made me pause mid-handful. "Was that your lame attempt at a joke?" I studied his profile, thinking the dark stubble only made the sharp angles of his face stand out more. Not wanting to get caught staring, I glanced at the steering wheel instead.

"I really do have three first names. Alexander Graham Graves, III, at your service," he said, his voice heavy with sarcasm. At least the guy knew how to make fun of himself. Maybe he wasn't a giant douchcanoe after all. "Everybody calls me Graves."

"Graves," I repeated, testing it out. It was weird, as far as names went, but it seemed to suit the dark and broody thing he had going on. "Sounds like the nickname a serial killer would have."

His lips quirked up. "Don't expect me to tell you where I hide the bodies."

"Why do I get the feeling you aren't joking?"

He laughed again, the deep sound washing over me. My stomach tightened, and I shook my head, feeling all over the place. Clearly, my blood sugar was still too low, and it was making me stupid. I poured more of the candy into my mouth.

He snorted. "You're a mess." His eyes flicked down my chest to my lap where a few M&M's had fallen. I plucked them from between my legs and stuffed them in my mouth too. His nose wrinkled in distaste.

"You forgot hot," I said, half-chewing while speaking.

"What?"

"Hot mess," I corrected.

Once more his eyes skimmed over me before turning back to the road. "Not sure that's the term I would use while you're covered in dirt and blood. Speaking of—does anything hurt?"

I stuffed another handful of M&M's in my mouth. The chocolate was cheap, but I didn't give a shit. Sugar in all forms was my kryptonite. "Nope."

He looked sideways again; this time incredulous. "Are you sure? How long ago did you crash? Maybe the adrenaline hasn't worn off yet."

I looked into the bag of M&M's, pressing my lips together. Did I want to tell him? Could I even lie?

"Salem," he prompted suspiciously. I gathered that I'd taken too long thinking.

"It was still light out when I crashed," I said slowly, stuffing another handful of tiny chocolates into my mouth so I had an excuse not to speak.

"That was like four hours ago," he said. "Why didn't you come up to the road during any of that time?"

"Well . . ." I trailed off, grabbing another handful. Cool fingers wrapped around my wrist before I could shove them in my mouth. I glared up at him.

"Hey, you said I could have them," I complained.

"I also asked you a question. Why were you still down there?" Only half his attention was on the road, and I was reminded of myself this afternoon, where I'd been too concerned finding the cupcakes to pay attention. Never mind that I'd also been speeding or driving like a bat out of Hell.

"Look, I don't want to talk about it," I said, avoiding the question because if I said that I died and came back to life without any injuries, he wouldn't exactly think I was sane. Or uninjured, since that sounds like something someone who had been hit upside the head might say.

Graves let out a tight breath. "I get that, but don't you find it a little odd that you were down there that long?" he asked, like I was on trial or something. All his questioning really did was bring my anger to the forefront once more.

"You know what I find odd?" I asked him. He lifted an eyebrow, silently urging me on. "What *you* were doing down there. Why were you in the woods with a flashlight to begin with?" I asked.

His lips pressed into a firm line and the muscle in his jaw ticked. "Looking for something," he answered vaguely.

I took the opportunity to lift both my eyebrows and lean in. "What were you looking for? Hmm?" I asked; or demanded, really.

"I was . . ." his words trailed off as if he were scrambling for them but didn't want me to see.

"Uh-huh, I thought so. You want all of my secrets, but you're hard-pressed to share any of yours. It's a two-way street, you know." I tugged my wrist out of his grasp and poured the rest of the candy in my mouth before crumpling the bag into a ball.

"What is?" he asked, sparing me another narrow-eyed glance.

"Trust."

He snorted. "I'm not the one with the trust issues. There are just some things that aren't mine to tell."

"Liar."

His grip tightened on the steering wheel, and I could hear the squelch of the leather beneath his skin. He was silent for so long I thought we were done talking, but after about a mile, he asked, "You ever heard of quid pro quo?"

I scrunched my nose. The expression was familiar, but I couldn't remember anyone actually using it in a conversation before. "I tell you something, you tell me something?"

He nodded.

"Sounds dangerous," I muttered, already missing my candy.

"The truth sounds dangerous to you?" he scoffed, his brow lifting in surprise.

"Less 'the truth' part and more the 'your reaction' part."

"Fine, let's try something easy. Why are you back in town, Salem?"

"My brother died. There are things I need to take care of here." It was the truth, but not all of it. It was, however, all I was going to tell him. Just because I was being honest, didn't mean I was spilling secrets.

He blew out a breath. "Couldn't you have a lawyer or someone take care of it?"

"Nuh uh," I started, then paused. "You don't get two in a row. It's my turn. What were you doing in the forest?"

"Patrol."

"Oh, come on. A one-word answer doesn't cut it."

"Maybe you should be more specific about the rules next time," he said, smirking.

Asshole. "Fine," I gritted out. "You're up."

"What caused the accident?"

I glared out the window, trying to recall the seconds leading up to the crash. "Something was in the road. I was speeding and overcorrected."

"Something?" he prompted.

"An animal, I think. It looked like it was on four legs. Hey, you owe me two now," I said, realizing I'd answered without thinking. "Why were you on patrol?"

"There've been some wild animal sightings recently. A group of us take turns checking traps that we set to see if we can catch it and relocate it outside of town."

I turned to face him. "Doesn't seem very smart to go after a wild animal on your own in the middle of the night without, like, a gun or vest or something."

"Was that a question?"

I blew out an annoyed breath, already reevaluating my stance that he wasn't a douchecanoe. He was at least half-douchecanoe. The other half still remained to be seen. "Fine. What kind of animal attacks?"

"Wolf," he answered.

I froze; my mouth already open with the words on the tip of my tongue.

Graves made a tsking sound. "My turn," he practically purred. "Why did you wait so long looking for help if you were fine?" he asked.

Mind still racing from his last answer, I spoke without thinking. "I think I died . . . you know, just a little."

Graves slammed on the brakes, coming to a dead stop in the middle of the road.

"Hey!" I shouted, my hands slamming on the dashboard. "I've already been in one accident tonight. No need to go for round two."

"You just told me you think you died!" Graves yelled, his hands dropping from the steering wheel.

"Yeah, well, you said you wanted the truth," I grumbled. "I know it sounds a little nuts, but I'm telling you the shit I saw before you got there . . ." My words died in my throat at the look on his face. "You think I'm crazy, don't you?"

Graves opened and closed his mouth twice before answering. "Run me through it from the beginning."

"What?" I protested. "You said quid pro quo—"

"And you just said you died," he interrupted, giving me a hard look. "I think I get to ask you anything I want right now."

I glared back at him, and the staring contest went on for all of five seconds before I grumbled, "Fine, but none of this will hold up in a court of law. You are not getting me committed for being straight with you."

A frown graced his too-perfect lips. "I'm not sure what I find more unbelievable right now. That you were digging around in your car—that was on fire—for Hostess cupcakes, that you think you died and came back to life, or that your biggest concern seems to be me trying to get you sent to a crazy house. Seriously, Salem? Just tell me what happened."

I took a deep breath and started talking. "I already told you; something ran into the road. It looked sort of like a wolf, but bigger, and it had red eyes. I swerved to avoid it and the car flipped. Everything went black . . . and then it didn't." I cringed, hating how absolutely batshit crazy I sounded.

"Keep going," he said, motioning for me to go on.

It was getting hard to meet his gaze, so I stared out the windshield. "I woke up, and there was this creepy girl. She looked like she belonged in the Addams family. She kept saying I had to go back and that it wasn't safe to stay there. When I looked over at the car, I saw my body was next to it on the ground. I touched it, and then I woke up looking like this." I gestured to myself. "The crazy part is, while there's blood everywhere, I'm actually fine. I can't find any wounds."

I waited for him to say something. Anything, really. When he didn't immediately start talking, I turned back to his glove box to see if there were more M&M's. My fingers barely brushed over the latch before he grabbed my hand.

I looked back at him, and there seemed to be some sort of decision he was weighing. "This is going to sound crazy," he started.

"I just told you I died and came back to life because a little girl told me to. So..." I let the words hang between us, and he finally nodded.

"Yeah. It does sound that way. Um, but you've been through a lot, and I'm pretty sure we haven't even scratched the surface of crazy yet. I'm pretty sure you did die, and that you did come back."

I blinked, evaluating him in a new light. Looks like I was going to have a roommate at the loony bin. "Okay . . . are you just saying that so that I feel better? Because if you're just trying to get in my pants—"

"Oh my God," Graves groaned. "Shepard said you were a bit extreme. Now I get it."

"Hey!" I slapped his hands away, and he visibly flinched. That made me feel a little bad. But just a little. "What's Shepard got to do with any of this?"

He exhaled heavily. "Well, if I'm right . . . everything. Salem, I don't know how to tell you this—"

"Just spit it out already."

"You say that . . ." he trailed off, looking at the car ceiling. "It won't be so easy to hear."

"I died in a car accident. Then I came back. I smushed my Hostess cupcakes that caused it—it doesn't get any harder than that, buddy." I crossed my arms over my chest.

"Smushing cupcakes is not equivalent to what I'm about to tell you," he said, utterly serious.

"I'm beginning to doubt that given you won't just say it. What's the big deal—"

"Magic is real. Fairy tales are real. Monsters are real." I stared at him open-mouthed, not sure how to respond. *Maybe I wasn't the only one to hit my head tonight . . .*

Then he said the craziest part of all.

"And I'm pretty sure you're one of them."

Scream

I STARED AT GRAVES FOR APPROXIMATELY THREE seconds before throwing my head back and laughing. I laughed so hard that my lungs ached and tears rolled down my cheeks. I could hear him swearing beside me, but couldn't seem to stop my laughter long enough to say anything. I mean, seriously, what other reaction was there?

"Oh man," I sputtered once I could catch my breath. "I really needed that."

He was stone-faced as he stared at me. "You done yet?"

I wiped a tear away and looked at him. He was livid. "Oh, come on, big guy. Don't tell me I managed to hurt your feelings. You tell me fairy tales are real and you expect me to what? Gasp? Faint? What reaction were you hoping for? Are you my prince charming? Did I come back to life because you woke me up with a kiss?"

From my vantage point, I could see a vein pulsing in his neck. He closed his eyes, the dark lashes tangling together as he took a deep breath.

"Not sure this is the time or place for meditation—"

His eyes flew open, and he glared at me. "Don't play stupid with me, Salem. It doesn't suit you." My mouth snapped shut. "I'll admit, I might not be the best person to give you the talk, but I'm what you've got, so you need to listen, and you need to listen well or you are about to find yourself in a world of shit you are not prepared for."

Something about the intensity in his stare had me nodding, my heart racing inside of my chest. "Okay," I managed, while inside I just kept thinking, *Oh, shit. He might be telling me the truth.*

Truth carries a certain weight to it. You know it when you hear it, and right now I was pretty sure Graves was about to bury me beneath a mountain of it.

"Farrow's Square is a supernatural town. *The* supernatural town, really. Almost everyone who lives here is somehow connected to the supernatural world—"

"But—" He glared at me and the words died on my lips. I ended up nodding for him to continue.

"Everyone. That doesn't mean they all know about the world they are connected to, but at least one person in their family is a supe."

"A supe?"

"A supernatural. Someone that isn't human," he said like it was nothing at all. This was just everyday life for him.

"What are you?" I asked, not sure I wanted to hear what kind of monster he thought I was just yet. That was a little more than I could handle on an empty stomach.

"The same thing as your brother, and your father, as it so happens. I'm a Grimm. A reaper. And I think you might be too."

"A Grimm reaper?" I repeated. "Like one of those

dudes that wears a cloak and has a scythe? Kinda like the villain in the *Scream* movie—"

"Oh my God," he groused. "I drop this bombshell on you and you're still going on about shit that doesn't matter—"

"Hey!" I snapped. "You're the one that sprung this on me. I just had the worst night of my life, died and came back, and now you're going on about monsters and how I may be one. What did you think I was going to do?"

"Well," he drawled, some of the ire in his voice fading. "I wasn't really sure. I've never had to do this before . . ."

"Clearly," I deadpanned. "You're not supposed to spring this shit on people when they're already on the verge of a meltdown, especially when they're without food. You at least try to ease them in. It's like foreplay. You have to preheat the oven before you just slide your dick right on in there."

Graves turned, blinked twice, and started talking before I could continue with my mixed metaphor. "I'm trying, okay? It's not exactly like I've done this before either. Fuck, before tonight I didn't even know it was possible for there to be female reapers."

"Didn't know it was possible?" I repeated. "If both my dad and brother were reapers—why the fuck didn't anyone tell me? I mean, Shep and I were twins for God's sake. That's a pretty big thing for them to keep from me and never consider I could be one too."

"Supernatural genetics doesn't work like other genes. Especially not the reaper one. Only males can be reapers. At least, that's how it's always been . . ." he trailed off.

"Yeah, well. Lucky me. I can't be in this town for one

goddamn second without crazy shit happening." I let out a tight breath and leaned back, closing my eyes. "Can you please keep driving? I'm disgusting and would kill for a shower and food right now."

"Yeah," Graves said, shaking his head. His foot eased off the brake, and we started moving once more. "Look, Salem. I know this is a lot to take in. Are you sure you want to go home right now? I know your aunt is probably expecting you, but if you go inside looking like you do now, she's probably going to take you to a hospital, and you can't tell them what you just told me."

I narrowed both eyes at him. "This is exactly what I meant by you being the fucking candy man with a van. I should have listened to my gut—and not the hungry one."

"For fuck's sake," Graves bemoaned, beating the palm of his hand against the steering wheel. "I'm trying to help you."

"How does telling me to lie to a doctor help me exactly?"

"Because one of two things will happen," Graves said. "You'll either get one that doesn't know anything and there's a large chance they'll think you're certifiable when there are no signs of a concussion or other head injury. Or —and I want to be clear that this is not the better of the two options—you'll get someone who knows something and suddenly the supernatural world is going to implode. Grimms aren't exactly popular around here."

"Mhmm." I swiped my tongue over my teeth. "So, let me get this straight, not only am I the weird dude from *Scream*, but in terms of the supernatural lottery, I just got the shit end of the stick. Lovely."

"Salem," he started.

"Graves," I shot back in an equally exasperated tone and then sighed. "Much as I think you probably belong in the crazy house with me right now, there's a small chance you might be right and not just trying to kidnap and rape or murder me. So . . ."

I lifted both eyebrows.

He shook his head. "You're incorrigible, and you're kind of a brat."

"Why, thank you," I said, mockingly sweet as I put a hand to my chest. "You're just a bushel of roses yourself, Stranger Danger."

"How is she his twin?" Graves asked himself under his breath.

I grinned at him. "If you only knew how many times I've heard that before." My smile faded a little at the reminder of my brother; of why I was home. "You're probably right. Esme can't see me like this. Even if I did manage to sneak into the pool house and shower, I still wouldn't have anything to change into. Everything I brought with me went up in flames with the car."

Graves blinked at me. "I think replacing your wardrobe is the least of your worries. I'll take you to my parents' house. You can clean up there and borrow some of my clothes. We'll figure out a game plan for what comes next while we're there."

"Uh, Graves . . . don't you think your parents might notice this?" I plucked at my blood-stained shirt.

Graves' eyes dropped to my chest, following my hand gesture, and he looked away, his knuckles white on the steering wheel. "They're out of town, and my brother lives at the frat house. There won't be anyone there to see you."

"Or to hear me scream," I muttered.

"How many times do I have to tell you—"

"Relax, killer. I'm just teasing you. But I'm telling you right now, you don't get to be little spoon."

"Salem," he said in annoyance.

I snickered. Getting Graves riled up was turning into my second favorite method of avoidance. As long as I was distracting myself with torturing him, the less time my brain had to think about the other, scarier things going on. Like the fact that I died. And came back. And that I was apparently some kind of Halloween freak show. Or that my brother was dead and I was here to find his murderer.

I closed my eyes and tipped my head back, wincing when I realized I was probably smearing blood into his upholstery. Fuck it. If I had to buy a new car, he could deal with getting his car detailed.

Graves and I fell into silence as he continued driving through town. My eyes flickered over the houses, watching old plantation homes give way to McMansions. Soon the houses were fewer, and more gates and twisting drives appeared.

Another ten minutes passed as he drove. Finally, he was turning up a well-lit drive, pausing only long enough to hit a button on his visor that sent a massive gate rolling open.

I leaned forward, curious despite myself about what his house would look like. I let out a low whistle as the sprawling mansion came into view.

"Cut the shit," he said. "We both know your place is twice this size."

"True," I said, "but size isn't everything. We both know it's what you do with it that matters." I glanced at him and waggled my eyebrows, emphasizing the double meaning in my words.

Graves groaned, cutting the engine and swinging his door open. "You are ridiculous. Come on. Let's get inside and get you cleaned up."

Whitewashed

I WRINKLED MY NOSE AT THE PAIR OF CLOTH slippers he dangled in front of me.

"Please don't ask. Just wear these until we can get you to a shower," he mumbled. I lifted both hands in surrender.

"Dude, I get it. I'm gross and you don't want to track it through the house. The part I'm judging is why you're wearing them too." I pointedly looked down at his cloth-covered shoes.

Graves sighed. "Because my mom is OCD," he said. "If we still had a housekeeper it wouldn't matter, but she doesn't like the way they clean. So, if either of us track shit in the house, and I clean it, she'll know." He lowered his head like the admission embarrassed him. Oddly enough, I found it more relatable than he realized and put the ugly ass painter's slippers on without giving him more grief.

He was really uncomfortable about it. At least he didn't have a really strange aunt with the weirdest quirks.

My aunt took the cake from them all.

Literally. One birthday she stole Shepard's and my cake

to see how well it would work if she stuck exploding fire-works in it.

Needless to say, not well. Unless you considered wearing your cake a good thing.

Graves opened the garage door leading into the house, and I followed. Perfectly white carpet led down a white-walled hallway, to—you guessed it—a whitewashed living room.

"I'm noticing a theme here," I muttered as we stepped past the pristine plastic-covered furniture. I side-eyed it like the couches were at fault for their current unpleasant state.

"Yeah," he said, completely unenthused as he led me across the house and up the stairs. "My mom likes things white. So she can see the dirt if it's there." His hand grasped the doorknob in front of us, and he let the door swing open.

I braced myself, somehow still expecting it to be a pigsty. I mean, I have been in college for the past four years. I've had boyfriends. I had a brother. Guys were disgusting.

But, Graves was the exception.

While the carpet was the same unblemished white as the rest of the house, his furniture was black and the bed comforter and drapes both gray. I stepped inside and took a whiff. Something subtle and masculine pervaded the air. I looked at him out of the corner of my eyes, standing there, hand scratching the back of his head awkwardly.

"You don't do this often, do you?"

"Nope." He shook his head. "Truth be told, I'm at the Gamma Rho house most of the time. It was dumb luck on your part I happened to be in the woods tonight."

"Dumb luck?" I repeated, crossing my arms over my

chest. "Do I need to repeat the night I've had for you to understand that nothing about this is lucky for me?"

"You know what," Graves said, moving to one of the two doors in his room as the light flicked on when he entered. He came out holding two fluffy black towels. "You're right," he said, handing them over. "Bathroom is right there. Why don't you go knock yourself out? I'll be downstairs in the kitchen."

I could see right through his ruse and instinctively knew he just wanted away from me for the time being. The feeling was mutual, though, and at the mention of the kitchen, I was even more motivated in getting clean so I could join him and hopefully find the snack cupboard.

Daydreaming about those Hostess cupcakes I stepped on, I moved into the bathroom and closed the door behind me with a nudge of my cloth-covered foot.

Setting the plush towels down on a white marble counter, I finally got a look at myself. "Sweet baby Jesus," I breathed, jerking back from my reflection. I'd thought I knew how bad it was because I'd seen myself splayed out in the woods, but I hadn't. Not really.

My hair was plastered to the side of my head, looking like a weird rusty pink helmet. The pieces that weren't matted together with blood and dirt were standing up in every possible direction, likely thanks to the wind. Dried blood and dirt crusted almost every visible inch of my skin, which only made my blue eyes look inhumanly bright as they stared back at me.

"Yeesh."

Turning away from myself, I stared at Graves' shower, trying to figure out how to turn it on. It was massive. Big enough for three Graves-sized dudes, with multiple shower-heads on each wall, and one rain-style showerhead centered in the ceiling. I peeled off my clothes, wincing when they took my arm hair with them, and moved into shower. I ran my hand along the wall until I felt the switch and turned the water on.

As I suspected, it was the perfect temperature. Neat trick.

Steam quickly filled the room as I stood under the hot spray, trying not to notice how the water immediately turned red. Knowing the only thing that was going to deal with these tangles was conditioner, I searched for a bottle. There weren't any.

Instead, there was an oddly-shaped box set into one of the walls with three silver buttons along the bottom. I'd seen something like this in a hotel once, so I was pretty certain the soap, shampoo, and conditioner were contained within. The only problem was it wasn't clearly labeled, so I had to test each one before I found what I was looking for.

Clean now, and smelling like Graves, I turned off the shower and wrapped myself in the towels. A quick scan of his room showed me he'd forgotten to leave out anything for me to wear, which meant it was time to snoop.

I didn't see a dresser, so I went back to his closet. Pulling the door open, I let out a soft chuckle. Graves' mom wasn't the only one with OCD. His closet was arranged by size and sorted by color. Not that it was hard, considering ninety percent of it was black. The other ten was denim. I made a mental note to buy him something bright. Maybe neon pink. Just to see his reaction.

Shaking my head, I wandered into the walk-in, noticing

the drawers along the back. I was tempted to pull on a pair of his black silk boxers, but resisted, settling instead for a black T-shirt and a pair of black sweats that I rolled up about seven times.

Finger-combing my hair, I found my cloth booties and left his room, following the sounds of clicking to the kitchen. The inside of Graves' home felt just as massive as the Shroud mansion I was supposed to be returning to tonight. My stomach twisted into knots as I thought of that, of the accident, of why I was home. Four years ago, I left it all behind: my name, my legacy, and especially my family—because my idiot brother was making the dumbest decision of his life and I refused to wait around until that decision killed him. Now it had. I was home. I wasn't just a Kaine anymore. I was a Shroud again. The thought unsettled me.

I walked up to the island in the center of the kitchen and took a seat on one of the barstools.

"Whatcha making?" I asked, peering over at his cutting board. Bright vegetables and leafy greens were cut and diced perfectly. He scooped it up in two handfuls and tossed it in the frying pan. It hit with a sizzle, and my stomach grumbled. On another burner, a pot of noodles was boiling.

"Spaghetti," he answered shortly, pushing the vegetables around the skillet.

"Right . . ." I drawled out. This was getting awkward fast. "Look, I'm sorry for kind of being a little bitchy tonight . . ."

"Just a little?" he asked, lifting an eyebrow.

I glared at him. "It's been a long night," I answered stiffly.

"Yeah," he sighed. "I've gathered that. It's just"—he paused, breaking the plastic on a pound of beef before dumping that in with the vegetables too—"it's been a long night," he settled on, repeating after me. "Have you told your aunt you're not coming home yet?"

"Shit," I cursed under my breath, pulling my phone from the baggy sweatpants. I typed out a quick text:

Staying at a friend's tonight. Be home in the morning. Love you. - Sal

"Annnnd done," I said, hitting send. Speaking of friends, I should probably reach out to Tamsin sometime soon too. That was a problem for tomorrow.

Tonight, I was busy having an early-twenties life and species crisis. I was allowed to avoid people. At least for a little while.

"You're going to have to tell her something, you know. I don't mind if you want to stay here tonight, but your car is totaled and you don't have any clothes, outside of mine." His eyes lifted briefly, scanning over me. I probably looked like a drowned rat, but that was better than a dead person. Something flared in his eyes, but I didn't get a chance to read it before it was gone and he was looking back at the frying pan.

"Yeah, I was thinking that maybe if you dropped me at my friend Tamsin's in the morning, she might be able to help me out with the clothes situation until I can order more. As for the car, I have to figure that out. I mean, we left it there. I don't want to lie to Esme, but if she sees it she's going to know why I didn't come home tonight and that I'm a liar." I twisted my hands in my lap, not liking that scenario. It was one thing to omit small parts of the truth for everyone's best interest. It was another thing to try to cover up a car accident that killed me.

"I'll take care of getting your car out of the woods. Leave that to me. Right now we need to figure out what kind of supernatural you actually are. Like I said, I think you're a female Grimm, as impossible as that is." He lifted the frying pan and did that thing where he flipped the food in the air and somehow it all stayed in the pan. Show-off.

Because I was a girl that loved through my stomach, seeing him in the kitchen cooking for me was oddly attractive. That could be because he was also hot. Like stupidly hot. Sitting here, clean and safe, it was impossible to ignore.

"Stranger Danger," I muttered under my breath, reminding myself not to go there. I was here because I died, and he wanted to help. That was it.

"What was that?" he asked, stirring something that was making my mouth water.

"Nothing. I was just going to ask how you planned to figure me out."

He shot me a questioning look.

"Figure out what kind of monster I am, I mean. Like is there some sort of test or . . ." I trailed off, completely out of my element.

Graves' attention was divided as he watched the food and answered my question. "Every supe has a trigger."

"A trigger?"

"Yeah, it's what unleashes their inner monster, so to speak. Vamps turn the first time they drink human blood, werewolves turn during the first full moon after they're bit, unless they're purebloods, but you get the idea."

"And Grimms turn when they die?" I guessed.

"When they die by supernatural means."

My face scrunched up in confusion. "What's supernatural about a car accident?"

Graves shrugged, taking something off of the stove and setting it on the counter beside him. "What caused it, maybe? Hard to say. But we can't really argue the fact that you died and came back, and the only supernaturals triggered by death are Grimms. So we're just going to have to take a leap of faith here."

I clasped my hands in front of me, leaning forward. "Alright, fine. I'm a Grimm. What does that mean? Am I supposed to feel any different?"

Graves' back was to me now, and I was a little distracted by the play of muscles beneath his shirt. "For reapers, it's a little different. We grow into our powers. It's not an all or nothing thing. Sort of like death kicked off the change, and now every cell inside you is evolving. Think of it like supernatural puberty."

"Great," I lamented. "As if this wasn't already enough of a party, let's throw in some acne and raging hormones."

Graves' shoulders moved with laughter. "No, it's not like that. More like you're going to notice that you can see better in the dark. You'll move faster; have more stamina. Those kinds of things, but it will build over time. You'll also notice that when you meet a supe, you're going to know what kind they are because you'll be able to see their soul."

"Wait . . . what?" I stammered. "You can see my *soul*? Shouldn't you be able to tell what I am then?"

"Well, I mean, everyone in a Grimm line looks the same. So there's no change there, unfortunately." Graves turned to face me again, leaning back against the counter. "Maybe it helps if you understand why reapers exist in the first place. Our abilities are all an extension of that."

"Are you telling me supernaturals have some sort of divine purpose?"

The side of his mouth lifted in a smirk. "Just Grimms."

"That's a hellofa pick-up line, Graves. Does it work on all the ladies? 'Hey baby, I'm a reaper and I was sent here by god'," I mimicked in an obnoxiously low tone.

Graves shook his head. "First of all, being a reaper is hardly a pick-up line. I already told you the supes hate us. Telling a girl isn't exactly going to get me into anyone's pants. If anything, it's harder because I'm a Grimm. Supes don't like us, and normal girls can't really handle super-strength the greatest . . . anyways, no one who isn't a supe is allowed to know what we are."

The thought of Graves and banging and super-strength had my mind going interesting places.

"Do all reapers have super-strength?"

"Yeah, all supes in general do. Some more than others. Grimms in general have the most strength, one of the fastest speeds, and better reflexes than the others." That seemed like quite the draw.

"Why are Grimms the special snowflakes?"

"We exist to keep the others in line."

"Like the police?" I asked.

"Pretty much," he answered, opening a can of tomato sauce and dumping it in. "It's a thankless job, but someone has to do it."

"Uh huh," I said. "You do know I'm not great with rules, right? Enforcing them? Probably not the greatest idea anyone's ever had." I tapped my nails on the counter and leaned forward, inhaling the aroma as the sauce began to boil. He flipped the burner off and stirred the veggies with a spoon.

"Well," he started, opening a cabinet and retrieving two bowls. "Fortunately for you, I don't think we should run around telling anyone. The Grimms aren't the most welcoming to begin with, and since there's never been a female, I don't know what kind of reaction we'd be looking at in the Brotherhood. Especially with everything else going on . . ." He drained the noodles in the sink behind him before portioning them out into the two bowls.

"Everything else?" I asked, not so subtly prompting him.

"Shepard's death, for starters," he said. "The funeral was only this afternoon. He's not the first Grimm who has died under mysterious causes in the past few years, as you know."

Awkward tension leaked into the conversation as he silently dumped meat sauce into both bowls before sliding mine across the counter. Graves opened a drawer and pulled out two forks, handing me one as he came to sit on the barstool beside me.

"When my dad died, they said it was an animal attack—even though my dad didn't believe in hunting," I said slowly. "When I got the call from my aunt that my brother died from the same thing . . . you gotta imagine this doesn't look great. Gamma Rho is what they both devoted their lives to. I always assumed it was just a frat before tonight. A crazy one, that asked way too much from its members, but a frat regardless. Now . . . I'm beginning to see that isn't all they are. Gamma Rho is just a front for Grimm Reapers." I stuck my fork in the bowl and twisted, wishing that it was the head of whomever killed my brother.

"You came back to figure out what happened," Graves said, nodding to himself. "I was in the woods tonight for the same reason."

I lifted my fork, then paused. "You told me you were checking traps."

"Yeah, for a wolf. Both your dad and your brother died from animal attacks. That wasn't a lie. We just left out that the animal was a werewolf and we can't seem to find the damn thing."

My mouth opened and closed. I looked between him and my bite of spaghetti. Starving as I was, I also sensed we were on the precipice of something. I dropped my fork and turned in my chair to face him completely.

"You're a Grimm," I said. "And it looks I am too. You want to find out who killed my brother. I do too. Are you thinking what I'm thinking?"

Graves looked like he stepped in something bad as he leaned away. "I don't know about this, Salem. You don't even know how to use your powers or anything—"

"So you'll teach me," I said, maybe a little too force-fully. "And then we're going werewolf hunting."

I Am Grace(less)

unreadable.

"What do you mean? It's practically our only option. If there's no one else we can tell for now, you train me and then—"

"I was talking about the hunting part. Of course I'm training you. But as you said, it's been a long night. You should eat and get some rest. We can talk about this more in the morning."

Having mostly won the battle for now, I let the subject drop and inhaled my food. It wasn't pretty. There were sounds coming out of me that usually only happened during what my aunt had dubbed "me time" during one awkward conversation a few summers ago. Graves was polite enough not to comment, and I was too satisfied to be embarrassed. I'd needed that meal more than I realized.

When I was finished, Graves was standing beside me holding out a napkin. "You've got a little something on your face," he said, lifting my empty bowl off the counter and putting it beside his in the dishwasher.

Taking the napkin, I swiped at my face. "Maybe I was saving it for later."

He rolled his eyes. "Cute."

"I know I am."

Graves snorted. "Keep telling yourself that."

I chuckled. The back and forth with him came so naturally. Most people couldn't handle my rough edges. Graves just sort of rolled with it, giving as good as he got. It was refreshing. Falling back into silence, I helped him load the dishwasher.

When the kitchen was immaculate once more, Graves led me back through the house toward his bedroom.

"In a house this big, you've got to be truly delusional if you think I'm sleeping in bed with you."

Graves shot me a pointed look over his shoulder. "I'm delusional? Who said anything about you sleeping in my room?"

"Uh, you're leading me to your bedroom."

"No, I'm not," he said, amusement flaring in his eyes. "There's a guest room two doors down the hall from mine. You'll sleep there tonight."

"Oh."

"Salem Kaine, at a loss for words. I didn't think I'd live to see the day."

"Please," I scoffed. "You've known me for, like, five seconds."

"That's all it took."

I rolled my eyes, but a smile was pulling at my lips.

We stopped outside a white door, Graves opened it and

then turned to me. "I was thinking, if we're going to be spending time together we're going to need a cover story. If you enroll in the university, it would give us a reason to be seen together."

"Do we need a reason?"

"If I keep dipping out to train you, my frat brothers are going to notice. They'll want to know where I'm going."

"Wouldn't it just be easier to tell people we're dating or something? That is something supernaturals in their twenties do, right?" It was an honest question. I didn't know anything about the dating habits of supes.

Graves shook his head. "Easier maybe, but not believable."

My eyes narrowed. "Why?"

"I don't date anymore, Salem. My life is too messy to bring someone else into it. So for me to start all of a sudden will only draw attention we don't need." He looked away uncomfortably, and I knew there was more.

"What aren't you saying?"

He ran a hand through his unkempt hair. "Your brother and I . . ." He paused, searching for words, but my stomach was already twisting in uncomfortable knots.

"I see," I said, sparing him the truth. Anytime a sentence started with 'your brother and I', well, I was smart enough to know where it was going.

Graves looked over, relief crossing his features. "You do?"

"Yup," I answered. "You swing for the other team. I'm guessing you're the boyfriend my aunt kept telling me about. 'The love of his life' and all that?"

His steady relief was quickly replaced with discomfort

as he shook his head. "No . . . that's Colin. He left town after the funeral today. I was Shepard's best friend. For me to be seen dating his sister right after he died..." He trailed off again, waiting for me to catch on.

"Oh." I wasn't sure how I felt about that. "Well, I suppose that makes sense. In some weird overly chivalrous universe where being my brother's best friend means you couldn't date me because of some stupid bro code where Shep can be the only man in my life. But sure, whatever." The longer I stood there talking to him, the worse that ache in my chest actually grew.

"Salem, it's"—he broke off, exhaling on a hard breath—"complicated. If you don't want to enroll in the university, we're going to have to find some other excuse. But for the time being, why don't we get some sleep? It's been—"

"A long night. Yeah. I know." I pushed past him into the guestroom. It was whitewashed the same as everything else in this house, but at least it was clean. "See you in the morning."

I was already closing the door behind me, more than ready to put this nightmare of a day to an end. The door was just about to click shut when I heard Graves, as clearly as though he were speaking in my ear, whisper, "Goodnight."

I pushed it the rest of the way closed, resting my weight against the cool wood as my eyes fell closed. There was little, if anything, about the night that I'd classify as good. But at least it was over. That would have to be enough for now.

"SALEM," a voice whispered.

It was that time of the morning when dreams blurred with reality, and I couldn't tell if I was still sleeping or awake. I was sprawled sideways on the bed, having performed some kind of sleep yoga in the middle of the night. One foot was jutting off the side of the bed, the other was cocked over the headboard, and both my arms were tangled above my head.

"Five more minutes," I grumbled, pulling my limbs into a tight ball and tugging the comforter up over my head.

The comforter started to slide down my body against my will. "Salem," the voice whispered again.

I groaned. "Fuck off, Graves. Don't you know better than to wake a girl up without at least bringing coffee?"

There was a snicker. A decidedly female snicker. I froze, suddenly wide awake. No one except Graves knew I was here. So who the hell was calling my name? My heart was beating wildly in my chest as I peeled my eyes open and sat up, warily scanning the overly bright room.

Not-Morticia was perched on the desk, looking like some kind of live-action gothic doll.

"What the hell are you doing here?" I breathed, pinching my leg hard to make sure I wasn't still sleeping. *Ouch. Okay, not dreaming, then.*

"We need to talk."

"I refuse to have any conversation that starts off that way. Especially without coffee."

"Salem—"

"Nope. Don't care."

Her placid expression didn't change, but something flashed in her dark eyes. Something that sent unease crawling down my spine. "Ignoring me isn't going to help you."

"I think we need to work on your definition of 'help' because ignoring my death hallucination seems like *exactly* what I should be doing."

"You know I'm not a hallucination, Salem."

"No," I said, finally moving to get out of bed and giving Not-Morticia a wide berth. "I do not know that."

"You need to be careful, Salem. They're going to be looking for you now. All of them. They will be drawn to you. Do not ignore them."

The familiar burn of anger was swiftly replacing any fear. "Who is 'they'? Look, if you want to be helpful, how about you try to go with something a little less cryptic?"

A small smile lifted her lips. "Our time is up. I'll see you soon, Salem."

She vanished in a puff of smoke and a knock sounded at the door. I let out a heavy groan.

"Salem?" Graves called. "Everything alright in there?"

I crossed the room to open the door. "Yeah, I'm fine—" I started when a door downstairs slammed.

"Alexander?" a female voice called out. Despite it not being my house, my family, or even my dignity on the line, I froze.

"Mom?" he called back incredulously. "What are you doing home?"

Footsteps sounded, coming up the stairs. My heart started to pound. I took one look at myself and knew that without a doubt, whatever his mom might have thought of my brother, seeing me in her son's clothes, pink hair tangled from sleep and teeth not brushed, was going to be a shocker if he never brought girls home.

I scratched the back of my head, looking between the door and the window across the room.

"Oh, your father had business to attend to. You know how it is," she said breezily. A slight tittering laugh that made me want to groan again came from a few feet away. "What are you doing here? I thought for sure you'd be with your brothers at the Gamma Rho house."

"I needed some space," he said, lying smoothly. I lifted both eyebrows, wondering where the awkward derp from last night went. "After Shepard..." His voice thickened with emotion.

Damn, he was a good liar.

I'd needed to remember that.

"Oh honey," his mother cooed. "Why don't we go to Freddy's for breakfast? I won't even tell your father."

"That sounds lovely, Mom. I just have to go help a friend with—"

I side-eyed the door, sensing a juicy admission coming. Leaning in, I carefully rested my ear to the wall. Or, at least, that was the plan.

Apparently all those super badass Grimm powers hadn't kicked in yet because it was more of a falling with style and stopping via wall, than a lean and listen kinda deal.

"What was that?" his mom asked. I sensed her eyes on the door and started backing up. Scrambling like crazy.

"What was what?" Graves asked. I could hear the annoyance in his tone that was aimed at me.

Glancing between the door and the window, I grumbled under my breath, "You owe me for this." If it were up to me, I'd rather get caught and chance her not liking me. But Graves didn't strike me as that type, and he did me a real solid last night.

In a swift motion, I slid the window open. It only squeaked a little.

There was only one problem.

The damn thing had a screen.

Blowing out a frustrated breath, I shoved at the center of the netting and the entire thing popped out.

Tossing the screen off the side of the house, I shimmied through and climbed out onto the three-foot stretch of roof beneath the dormer window. My bare feet gained purchase with the scratchy roof panels, but my muscles protested. After all the crap yesterday, I was whole, but sore. And not in the good way.

I was only just sliding the window closed as the doorknob started to turn.

I threw myself against the side of the house, squeezing my eyes shut like that would keep them from seeing me. Sighing at my stupidity, I held my breath, praying they were in and out quickly.

"Mom—" Graves' exasperated tone was cut off, silence swelling until he said, "I told you I didn't hear anything."

"Hmm," she murmured. "So how do you explain this?"

My eyes flew open. Explain what?

"Explain what?" Graves said, echoing my own confusion.

"The bed was obviously slept in," she said.

Good luck with that, buddy. But he didn't need my luck. I'd already forgotten he was a master liar.

"I was a little drunk last night. I slept in here by mistake."

"Ah, sweetheart. That's nothing to be ashamed of. You buried your best friend yesterday. Come on; let's go to Freddy's. Some food will make you feel better."

I could hear the shuffling of feet as they made their way to the door, and I felt my body relaxing, my breath leaving me in a whoosh. But I should have known better than to relax. I'd more than used up any luck I had in the bank during yesterday's resurrection.

The sound of Justin Timberlake's crooning filled the silence. *Oh, for fuck's sake.* In the chaos, I'd completely forgotten about my phone or that it was now giving away my location.

Tamsin, your timing sucks, I mentally griped, recognizing her ringtone. Knowing it was officially time to get out of Dodge, I started creeping for the edge of the roof. I was on the second floor, but there were more than enough trees surrounding the house to make that a non-issue. It wouldn't be the first time I'd snuck out of a house. With the way things were going, it probably wouldn't be the last either.

Reaching the edge, I swung my legs over, my toes stretching to touch the closest branch. Once I made contact, I rolled onto my stomach, Graves' shirt snagging on the rough roofing. The sound of voices was getting louder, but I couldn't make out any words over the pounding of my heart.

With a muffled groan, I eased myself onto the branch, feeling the scratch of the roof against my bare skin. I hissed in pain as I moved onto the tree, looking down only long enough to see the tears in my shirt.

Great. More blood.

Ignoring the sting, I scrambled down the tree, channeling my inner wild child and praying I didn't break my neck. Somehow I didn't think the whole coming back to life thing would happen a second time. And I really didn't want to put that theory to the test.

I hit the ground with a soft plop, twigs and rocks digging into my bare feet. I was swearing up a storm, trying to walk as carefully as I could when I heard the door open.

"Motherfucker. Give me a break," I hissed, diving into a bush.

Cat burglar I was not. This was getting ridiculous. I hadn't even had coffee yet, and I'd already been through the wringer. If this was what my life was going to be like now that I was a Grimm, I seriously wanted to find someone I could talk to about giving it back.

"Why don't I drive, honey?" Graves' mom said, leading him arm in arm to an Audi R8. My jaw dropped, and it had more to do with the car than the fact that they were barely strapped in when she took off like a bat out of Hell.

Where my brother enjoyed rebuilding cars, the way they became my crutch had little to do with the joy of fixing them up and more to do with the speed behind the wheel. Everyone had a crutch. Something they knew they shouldn't like or do. Mine was food and fast cars.

As far as I was concerned, there were worse things to love.

Though I should probably reevaluate that given it was my driving that got me into this mess in the first place.

As soon as the R8 cleared the end of the driveaway, I got to my feet and called Tamsin back.

The phone rang once before she picked up.

"Salem! Where have you been—"

"Look, I got into some trouble. I'm going to need you to pick me up at the Graves' mansion ASAP."

Silence greeted me on the other end of the phone.

"Graves?" Tamsin repeated.

"Yup," I answered, waiting for the onslaught. Keys jingled in the background. A car door slammed shut. Spice girls started blaring in the background.

"I'll be there in ten," Tamsin said.

"Okay, see you—"

"And Salem—you better be ready to tell me what the fuck happened and why you're hanging out with Shepard's best friend."

The line went dead. I couldn't decide if I was lucky that I had a friend who would pick me up with zero notice, or unlucky because I couldn't lie for shit.

Sex Vampire

A GRAY PORSCHE PULLED UP NEXT TO THE CURB outside the Graves' front gate. The car came to a full stop, and Tamsin rolled down the window.

"Hop in, loser," she called, quoting *Mean Girls*.

"Oh my God," I grumbled, climbing into the passenger seat. "You're still doing that?"

"Just for you, babe," she said, smiling perfectly. Who was I kidding? Everything about Tamsin was perfect. Her white smile. Her chocolate-colored skin. Her dark, wavy hair and golden eyes were accentuated with her perfect makeup skills. I leaned over, twisting in my seat to hook my right arm around her shoulders and pull her close.

"I missed you," I said. "LA is great, but it's not the same without my best friend."

"Back at you, asshole," she said, embracing me tightly.

We pulled apart, and she clasped my shoulders. "Now, you look like crap, and I'm picking you up from the Graves' mansion—where I'm pretty sure you slept your first night back in Farrow's Square. Anything you wanna tell me?" she prompted, smiling again.

My happiness at seeing her fizzled out because one thing with Tamsin and I was that we never, ever lied to each other. Not that I was great at it anyways. While blunter with me, she was the honey to my vinegar. Which kinda said a lot about how much of an asshole I was when I thought about it.

"Want to?" I hedged, sitting back in my seat.

She answered by lifting one perfectly sculpted brow. "Spill it."

I blew out a breath, trying to figure out where to even start when something Graves said the night before came back to me. Tamsin grew up in Farrow's Square. If everyone was somehow connected to the supernatural world, that meant my bestie was no exception. But did she know . . .

"What do you know about supernaturals?" I asked her, staring her straight in the eye.

I was expecting her to laugh, or to brush off the question. What I was not expecting, in any universe, was for her to groan.

"Oh, shit. I was hoping we'd never have to have this conversation." She studied me carefully, seeming to appraise my appearance in a new light. "Do you want to start or should I?"

"Me? It looks like I wasn't the one keeping secrets, Tam. So why don't you tell me how it is I only learned that monsters were real yesterday, and my question doesn't seem at all shocking to you."

She shrugged. "I didn't *want* to keep it from you, Salem.

It's kinda rule number one, though. We aren't allowed to talk about it with people who aren't . . ." she trailed off, shaking her head. "I'm a succubus," she finally blurted. She looked like she was waiting for me to jump out of the car and take off down the street. Which said a lot because I don't run. Literally. I've probably ran like three times in my life.

I blinked at her, not familiar with the term. "What's that? Some kind of fairy or something?"

She laughed, shaking her head. "No. Not a fairy. I guess you could say I'm like a sex vampire."

"A what now?" But even as I asked the question, it made a weird sort of sense. Tamsin had always been drawn to men. It didn't matter if they were single, married, or didn't bat for her team, they couldn't seem to get enough of her as soon as she opened her mouth. I'd chalked it up to my best friend being supermodel hot, but maybe it was something else.

"Succubi feed off of sexual energy. We need it to survive."

"That . . ." I trailed off, trying to think of the right words, "sounds like fun?"

Tamsin laughed, looking relieved. "It can be. It can also be a giant pain in the ass. But enough about me. It's your turn."

"Well, I'm not sure mine is as easy to explain . . . you ever heard of a Grimm?"

She snorted, her expression going dark. "Those power-happy ass clowns? Who doesn't know about the Grimms?"

Her reaction had me faltering. Graves wasn't lying when he'd said people hated his—err, our—kind. "Um, well. Looks like I am one. Surprise," I added weakly, doing little jazz hands when she didn't speak.

"Come again?" she said, leaning closer.

"I bet you say that to all your meals," I said, attempting to break up the tension.

Tamsin didn't break a smile. "I knew that it ran in your family. I mean, obviously I knew about your brother and father, but I didn't think . . . there's never been . . ." she trailed off, her eyes widening as a thought occurred to her. "Salem, did you *die* last night?"

"Uh . . . kinda?"

"You bitch! And you didn't call me?"

"And say what, exactly? I didn't even know supernaturals were a thing, how was I supposed to know you weren't going to have me committed?" She opened her mouth to reply, but I waved her off. "It doesn't matter anyway. Graves found me before I had a chance to do anything."

"Found you?" she asked. "Where were you? What happened? I knew I should have called when you didn't show up for the funeral. I just sort of assumed it was you, and—"

"I was skipping the funeral either way." I sighed. "About half an hour out from the house, an animal ran into the road and I swerved to avoid it but flipped my car. I woke up a few hours later in the woods. Graves found me digging through the wreckage for Hostess cupcakes." I lowered my head in both hands and scrubbed them down my face.

"Are you serious right now?"

I dropped my hands into my lap and glared over at her. "Do I look like I'm joking, Tamsin?"

"Well, I had to ask," she said, defensively. "I mean, you

can't tell me that doesn't sound a tiny bit crazy, even for you."

"The dying part?" I asked. "Or the—"

"The fucking cupcakes. Dude, *you died*, and your biggest concern was finding food? I'm not sure if I should be laughing right now or not. Why didn't you just call someone?"

You know, when she put it like that, it really did give the situation a bit of perspective.

"Speaking of cupcakes. Any chance you brought me anything . . ." My words dried up at the withering look on her face. "Alright, I'll take that as a no. You're forgiven. This time. Because I called last minute. But next time—"

"Put your seatbelt on," she said. "I'm starting to see how you ended up with Graves. Did he offer you food?"

"There were M&M's in the car," I said, knowing I should probably feel some shame about it, but unable to find the fucks I never had to begin with. I clipped the seatbelt and the car started moving.

"Have you eaten anything this morning?" she asked like the amazing best friend she was. "And where is that dickhead now? You look like a hobo, Salem."

I looked down at my torn shirt and baggy pants. "Yeah, I kinda do. It's not his fault, though." I scratched the top of my head, and it occurred to me, I needed to do something about my hair as I pulled a stray leaf out of the tangled strands. "His mom came home this morning, so I snuck out the window and climbed down a tree, sort of. It was more falling than climbing, but whatever. Anyways, I hid in a bush until I could call you. Great timing, by the way. Your ringtone almost gave me away."

"Did it ever occur to you to just act like a friend sleeping over?" she asked.

"Apparently Mr. Three First Names doesn't have friends, or girlfriends, or is friends with girls outside the whole Gamma Rho sausage fest," I said. Tamsin snorted. "He thinks people will question us hanging out if I don't go back to attend the university, but I finished like six months ago, and this is your last semester."

"Well, he's got half of a point. The thing he overlooked is that you're Shep's sister. If he starts hanging out with you, most people will write it off as him helping you through a rough time. Even Gamma Rho." She sped down the highway before taking the exit into town.

"You think? Because I don't want to go back to school. College was hard enough the first time I did it. Accelerated semesters or not." I paused, eyeing the McDonald's as we passed it and debating how much I was willing to sacrifice for a Big Mac. "Any chance we can stop somewhere—"

"We're not stopping anywhere with you looking like that. I'm taking you back to the house. Sigma Upsilon actually stands for Succubus United. Surprise," she said sarcastically as she pulled onto University Drive. "Luckily for you, cooking is a succubus thing. They were already starting on breakfast when I left to get you."

My mouth watered just thinking about it. "Have I told you lately how much I love you, Tam?"

She smiled a little. "Never hurts to hear it."

"Well, I do," I said with an emphatic little nod as she found a parking spot on the street. "Is there anything else I need to know about succubuses?"

"Succubi," she automatically corrected. "And no, not

really. I mean as a general rule we don't tend to have a filter, especially when it comes to sex, but neither do you. No one is going to try anything if that's what you're worried about."

"No, that's not what I meant. It's just this is all new to me. I don't want to accidentally put my foot in my mouth, ya know?" I asked, stepping out of the car.

"When has that ever stopped you before?"

"Okay, good point," I said, following her up a narrow walkway.

"Just keep an open mind and all will be well. I think we'll be able to find you something a little less hobo chic for you to wear as well."

"Bless you," I said as she swung the door wide open and gestured for me to come inside.

"Welcome to the Sigma house, Salem." The smell of bacon hit my nose first, followed by coffee and vanilla. "The kitchen's that way," Tamsin said, gesturing to my left. "You might want to wipe the drool off your chin, though."

I glared at her and followed my nose to the kitchen. Tamsin knew me well enough to know I was going to be miserable to be around if I didn't get something in my stomach ASAP. Ever since I was a kid I'd been that way. Shep always said I needed to stop eating my feelings. I told him if he ever tried to take food away from me again, I was going to have a sister instead of a brother.

She followed close behind me, waving to a blonde with a pixie cut standing at the stove. "Mandy Jane, this is Salem."

The girl's smile wavered as she turned to greet me, her

eyes widening slightly as she took in my appearance. "Walk of shame?" she guessed.

I snorted. "You could say that."

"Help yourself to the coffee. It's a fresh pot."

"You guys are angels," I breathed, wasting no time filling a mug. Tamsin was ready with the creamer, handing it to me before I needed to ask. "Thank you," I murmured after the first delicious sip.

Mandy Jane had a plate of blueberry pancakes and a side of bacon waiting for me on the table. "Dig in," she said.

I'm not sure if it was the food or being around Tamsin, but I was feeling more at ease than I had been for a while. It felt like I could breathe again.

I didn't look up until my plate was clean, blushing a little when I realized I was practically deepthroating my fork trying to get the last of the syrup off of it. "Uh . . . that was delicious."

Mandy Jane beamed at me. "There's plenty more if you want seconds."

"She'll go into a coma if she eats anymore," Tamsin answered for me before I could accept.

I might have pouted, but I didn't contradict her. I'd already had four pancakes and six pieces of bacon. I'd be good for a few hours.

Probably.

"So, Salem," Mandy Jane said, sipping her own mug of coffee, "you going to tell us about the guy that left you looking like roadkill this morning?"

"Interesting choice of words," I muttered to myself.

"Either he was amazing, and I want to know everything, or it was so bad you had to escape before he woke up, and I still want to know everything. So which is it?" she asked, her green eyes sparkling with laughter.

Two more succubi walked in, saving me from having to immediately respond.

"Hey, Tam," one of the girls wearing a multi-colored beanie and with cornrows down to her back said. "Who's your friend?"

"Tanya, this is Salem." Tamsin grabbed my forearm and pulled me next to her. "Salem, this is Tanya and Kayla. Tanya was my big when I first pledged."

"Hi, nice to meet—"

"Girl, you reek of being horny and unsatisfied," Tanya said, dropping all small talk. She snapped her fingers twice. "Tell your new friend Tanya what happened."

She started to come forward, and Tamsin stepped in front of me. "Actually, Salem has been through a really rough time. I'm going to take her back to my room and help her pull herself together."

Tanya half-frowned but shrugged and let it go. "You just give us a call if you ever need some *help* with that situation, Salem." She and Kayla waved as Tam pulled me down the hallway.

She dragged me into the last door on the right and closed it shut behind us.

"Okay," Tamsin said. "So, there's one thing I might have forgotten to mention to you."

I crossed my arms over my chest and lifted an eyebrow. "And that is?"

"No one here can know you're a Grimm. No one anywhere, really. Graves might have told you we sort of hate the Grimms here. What he didn't tell you, I imagine, is why."

I shrugged, letting my arms drop away as I took a look around her room. Clothes were strung across the floor. Her bras hung off the bed posts. Half a leftover pizza was sitting on the end table and beside it was a bowl of condoms. Not used. Thankfully.

"He said they're like the police," I said, returning my eyes to her.

"That's surprisingly accurate," Tamsin said with a frown. "Here's the deal. For the last several hundred years, reapers have been the self-appointed enforcer of supernatural rules and laws. Like all self-appointed pricks, the power went to their heads. Right now, you're in the middle of what basically amounts to a turf war. Supes are dying because of reapers, and reapers are dying from what we assume is probably supe retaliation. The whole point of me explaining this is that if anyone knows you're a reaper, they're going to shun you. However, the reapers are misogynistic assholes and not likely to claim you. It's a shit situation to be in, especially when you don't understand your powers. At all."

She paced back and forth, talking an awful lot about shit I didn't know an awful lot about. Fortunately for me, she used small words.

"So basically, no one wants me, and even though I'm now part of this world, I don't fit anywhere?" I asked, unable to keep the sulk out of my voice.

"Yes. No." She groaned and then grabbed my arm again, pulling me down onto the bed beside her. "It's complicated. What really needs to happen is you, me, and Graves need to sit down and have a heart-to-heart—so then you can make a semi-educated decision on how you want to handle this. You have options, but all of them have consequences that you don't know enough to fully understand."

"I already know what I want to do. Graves is going to train me to be a badass reaper, and then I'm hunting down the bastard that killed my brother. What's there to talk about?"

Tamsin stared at me for a second before shaking her head. "It's almost sweet how fucking naive you are right now. Girl, you may *think* that this is straightforward, but you have no idea what you have just gotten yourself into. It's not that black and white."

Before I could open my mouth to grill her further, the sound of shouting down the hall brought us both to our feet.

"Not again," Tamsin whined, throwing the door open so we could peek our heads out.

At the other end of the hall, a very naked man was stumbling out of a bedroom. "Laura! Laura, come back!" He was shouting, tears running down his face. "Don't leave me. I need you. Baby, please. I'll do whatever you want."

"Fuck," Tamsin said, leaning against the doorframe while other succubi flooded the hall.

"Damnit, Laura," Kayla said as she stomped down the hallway. "You can't keep doing this shit. Enthralling is an executable offense. Are you trying to get us all killed?"

"Executable?" I whispered, my eyes wide as I glanced at Tamsin.

She nodded.

A tall, Bettie Page look-a-like popped out of another

door. "Shit. I didn't mean to. I must have gotten carried away. I'll take care of it." She strutted down the hall to the still sobbing man. "Jake. Jake, look at me."

He fell to his knees and started kissing the tips of her polished boots. "I don't deserve to look at you. You're a goddess, I'm just your slave."

"I wasn't asking, slave," she growled, her voice a sexual purr. Even I wasn't immune to the web of seduction she was weaving around him. Desire coiled low in my belly, and I shifted uncomfortably as my nipples grew hard.

"What is happening?" I muttered, crossing my arms over my chest to try and stave off my unwanted reaction.

"She's charming him. It's Succubus 101. We can make our prey feel whatever we want them to. Desire. Need. Even fear."

"Fear?" I asked. "I thought you guys just wanted sex."

"Ever heard of a sadist?"

I grimaced, looking at FemDom Laura in a new light. "Are you saying that's not consensual?" Given the way Jake was standing to attention—in both ways—it certainly didn't look like he was unwilling, but watching the rapid shift of his emotions, it was hard to tell.

"Eh . . . it's a gray area. Most supe powers are, but succubi more so." Tamsin lifted a shoulder. "The guy is begging for it; it's his scene. But we've been taught to only use our powers to enhance the pleasure for both parties, even though we can actually do a lot more. It's easy for us to accidentally overdo it when feeding. But when prey get addicted and can't function without, we call it the thrall. It comes from them being addicted, but it creates a dependency that isn't healthy and long-term tends to fuck with their heads too much. This isn't even a bad case of it."

I gaped. *Not a bad case?*

Watching Laura manipulate the man before her, crooning and whispering things only he could hear, I suddenly understood why it was an executable offense. These women were capable of taking away someone's free will.

A shudder worked its way down my body. I had thought I understood what Tamsin was. It'd seemed straightforward enough, but seeing the evidence of what succubi could do . . . she really was a monster. A beautiful one, but no less dangerous because of it.

"Annnnnd that just proves my point," Tamsin said as we watched the poor sucker follow Laura back into her room in a daze. Giving me a gentle shove, she pushed me back into her room and shut the door.

Maybe Tamsin was right. I really didn't have a clue about this new world I was a part of. "Alright," I sighed. "So what do you want me to do? Call Graves and invite him over here for dinner or something?"

Tamsin's eyes went wide. "God no. Don't invite him here. Jesus. Were you listening to anything I said?"

"So where, then? Where can a succubus and two reapers go without raising any suspicion?"

"Your house," Tamsin said immediately. "The sooner, the better. You should probably call Esme and tell her you're having company for dinner. And text your man and tell him the plan."

"I, uh . . . I didn't get his number."

Tamsin rolled her eyes. "Okay, I'll work on that. You go

take a shower. I'll leave something out for you to wear." She was already moving—a one-woman tornado—as she started pulling things out of her closet. I was making my way to the door when she called me back. "Salem?"

"Yeah?"

"I'm really glad I didn't lose you too. Even if you are a dirty soul-stealer now." I could hear the throb of pain in her voice and knew she meant it, insult aside.

"Back at you, sex vampire," I said, chest getting tight.

She threw a purple thong at my face, ruining the moment. "Now get out of here. You smell like you got it on in a barn. I would know."

"WHAT DO YOU MEAN HE STILL HASN'T responded?" I sighed, running a hand through my clean hair. I stretched my shoulder, not caring for how tight the T-shirt of Tamsin's was on my body. We were both pretty thin, but I had five inches on her, and it showed in the form of the shirt not covering my pale ass stomach. At least it was early September and I wouldn't freeze my ass off in clothes a size too small.

"Well, I texted him once Tanya's friend's brother's cousin gave me his number. I was just asking him to meet up, and he hasn't responded. I'm wondering if something is going down at the Grimm house today. I know they have a frat party like every other night, but this is weird—no one ignores me." She flipped her long, dark hair over one shoulder and then picked at her nails.

"Okay, how about this—I'll swing by the Grimm house to get him." I paused to pull my phone out of my back pocket. Using the tip of my thumb, I bent one corner of the case back and grabbed my credit card, thanking my lucky stars that I kept the important cards in my phone case and not in a wallet like a normal person. "You're going to go to the nearest store and get me a bunch of clothes and shit and put it in a suitcase—then meet Graves and me at my place, where I'm going to pretend that I got rid of my beautiful BMW for some stupid reason and act like I didn't just lose all my favorite shit in a car accident. Sound good?"

She took one look at the credit card and asked, "Do I have a spending limit or—"

"Just be reasonable. I don't need Louis Vuitton purses or Jimmy Choo pumps. I need clothes that look somewhat normal and fit me, and a sturdy pair of Docs." I pointedly looked down my body and then lifted an eyebrow in her direction.

She took my card and nodded once. "Got it. Anything else?"

"Nope. Let's do this."

She opened her bedroom door, and we let ourselves out the back, avoiding interacting with the other succubi. While they seemed like perfectly nice people, I also just got a front-row seat to a leather-clad dominatrix trying to un-brainwash some rando from thinking he was her sex slave.

I shuddered to think what they might do to me if they knew what I really was, and then I decided that was a problem I'd worry about if we ever came to it. Right now they thought I was Tamsin's weird hobo friend that ate a lot, which suited me just fine. It wasn't that far off, actually.

Outside, Tamsin hopped in her Porsche with one last sarcastic salute, and then it was just me standing on the sidewalk of a school I didn't even go to. I tried to hook my thumbs in my pockets as I started walking toward the

Gamma Rho house, but the itty-bitty booty shorts were closer to underwear than anything else.

Giving up on that, I walked up the hill breathing just a little heavier than before, and I stopped at the bottom of the stairs. I stared at the two-story brick house, awkwardly tugging my shirt down, but it only flashed more cleavage. As a result, I was ninety percent sure I looked like a hooker, but considering I was heading into a frat house, maybe that was a good thing.

I climbed the stairs and stood in front of black double doors. There was an old Victorian-style door knocker, but I wasn't sure if anyone would actually hear it, so I opted for the doorbell off to the side instead.

I could still hear the electronic chiming when the door opened, and a guy built like a lumberjack stared down at me. His eyes immediately dropped to my chest. Score one for the cleavage.

"Can I help you?" he asked, not bothering to meet my eyes.

"Hi, I'm Shep's sister. I'm here to see Graves."

That caught his attention. His eyes moved up my body, making me feel like I needed my third shower in less than twenty-four hours. "You're Salem?" He smirked, leaning against the door. "What you need Graves for?"

There was a scuffle behind him, and the perv looked back, giving me time to twist and poke myself in the eye with the corner of my nail. Tears immediately welled, and I spun back just as he did.

"He's"—I sniffled—"helping me . . . with . . . my brother's things." The tears were openly streaming, and the linebacker was clearly uncomfortable. I gave a mental eye roll.

So predictable. One thing all macho guys had in common was their inability to handle a crying girl.

"I'll, uh, just go get him for you. Graves!" he shouted into the house. "Get your ass down here and deal with this."

I had to work hard to keep my sad girl act going as a flicker of anger ignited within me. What did the asshole mean, 'deal with this?' He was only the second reaper I'd met, and so far, I was not impressed with my species. Hopefully, the others wouldn't be quite so douchey.

I couldn't help but notice he didn't welcome me into the house either. The guy was probably afraid all my girl cooties would infect his super-macho frat house. *Jerk.* So I was still standing on the porch when Graves came down the stairs.

"Salem?" Graves asked, looking equal parts furious and concerned as he rushed to the door. "I've got this, Samuel," he said under his breath, pushing the other guy out of the way and stepping outside with me. "Is everything okay?"

As soon as the door shut behind him, I started to rub my eyes. "I poked myself in the fucking eye and it hurts."

"What the—why the hell would you do that?" he said.

"Because I needed to cry so that the lumberjack that answered the door wouldn't ask me more questions about why I needed to see you. I don't know how to cry on command. Why are we even still talking about this?" I ran a hand through my shoulder-length hair. "Why were you ignoring my texts?"

"Your texts?" he trailed off, and then his blue eyes flared wide. "That was you?"

Uh-oh. I knew I shouldn't have let Tamsin be the one

to talk to him. "Well, I mean. It was Tamsin on behalf of me."

Graves pulled his phone out, clicking something on the screen and holding it out for me to read. "Would *you* have responded if you got that?"

My eyes dropped to the little gray bubbles that read:

Yo, Graves, wanna fuck?

You should really tap this . . . at my place . . . tonight.

I'm thirsty for your scythe. You feel me?

I only made it halfway down the screen when I'd seen enough to understand. I scrubbed a hand through my hair. "Okay, I'm just going to start by saying that you're a fucking idiot if you thought that was me. Thirsty for your scythe? Really? Now, onto point two—"

"Are you really doing this right now?" Graves demanded, grabbing me by the arm and pulling me down the stairs.

"Doing what?" I asked, shrugging him off with relative ease. "Tracking your ass down after you left me to climb out your window because you didn't want your mom to know I slept over?" I gave him a pointed look, and he lowered his head a fraction. "Which, by the way, you owe me for."

"You know, while it was nice of you to help cover for me in the moment, reminding me that I owe you isn't how you convince people to do things for you, Salem," he said. "Also, I'm not talking about that. I'm referring to you trying to defend the slew of texts I got an hour ago that sound ridiculous. If I wasn't looking at you right now, I'd think you were high when you sent these."

"If you'd let me finish I would have told you my best

friend is apparently a succubus and more than a little horny, and *she's* the one that texted you; not me. Now, as for the whole 'nice' thing. You wanna know what's *not* nice?" I asked, not giving him a chance to respond. "A girl telling you she died, you tell her she's a mythical monster, and then disappearing when your mommy comes home. I need to figure out what the fuck I need to be doing right now so that I can find my brother's killer. Werewolf or not." I poked him in the chest, and Graves took a step back to catch himself. Both his hands came up to grab my arm, warm fingers touching my skin.

"You said a lot of things I want to respond to, but we're going to start with the obvious," Graves said, lowering his voice. "Who did you tell? It's been twelve hours since we had that whole conversation about how Grimms aren't very popular." His face somehow went from being very punchable and far away, to only inches from mine.

I opened and closed my mouth, throat suddenly dry. "You left me at your place with no instructions. I called my best friend and because I'm not a liar I told her the truth when she asked what happened. But don't worry, she's a succubus—"

"Yeah, I got that part. They get in trouble at least once a semester for fucking with the humans on campus. Not exactly a great species to tell this sort of secret to when their entire house spreads lies like chlamydia."

Okay, he was back to being punchable again.

"Tamsin is like my sister. She wouldn't say anything that would put me in danger."

"Oh yeah?" he asked, and I sensed the asshole comment coming from a mile away. "When did she tell you she was a succubus? Because as of last night you were telling me that you knew nothing about this world. So who's the liar here?"

"You're a massive dick, you know that?"

Graves' eyes narrowed, and he leaned a little closer. "I might be a dick, but right now, I'm the only person you know who can actually help keep you alive. You need to remember who your allies are, Salem. You can't just go around—"

"I'm not *just* anything. She is my best friend, who I've known since I was eleven, by the way. You are barely more than a stranger to me, so excuse me if out of the two of you, my trust is on team Tamsin. Maybe she lied by omission, but she did it because she had to. As soon as she knew she could, she told me everything."

He made a noise that sounded suspiciously like a growl. He looked away, a vein pulsing hard in his neck. "If you don't trust me, then why are you here?"

"I've been trying to tell you that," I said, beyond exasperated. "Tamsin wants the three of us to get together tonight at my place to talk through what I need to know and what my next steps should be to keep me safe. You guys may not think much of each other, but you both seem to agree that I am about one breath away from getting myself killed . . . again. I'd like to avoid that if possible."

Graves looked back at me, his eyes hard. "Fine."

"Fine? Really?" I was a little shocked he'd actually agreed. I thought for sure I was going to have to bribe him.

"Yes, Salem. Really. Despite what you think, I'm not going out of my way to be an asshole here. All I've been trying to do since I found you yesterday—"

"I'm not a stray puppy, Graves."

His eyes went frosty, but he continued to speak over me "—is to get you as up to speed as I can and keep you safe. This is new territory. For both of us," he added, lowering his voice as if he just remembered there was a house full of reapers a few feet away. "We need to work out a training schedule, and there's still a lot I haven't had a chance to tell you."

I let out a little groan, my brain already overloaded with everything him and Tamsin had dumped on me. "You guys and your secrets. You know, none of this would be an issue if everybody just told the truth from the beginning."

Graves snorted. "No one really wants to hear the truth all the time."

"I do," I said.

"Oh yeah? You'd really be okay with me telling you that in those clothes you look like you're about to audition for a porno?"

My mouth fell open.

"Exactly," Graves said, noting my reaction. "Just because something is true doesn't mean it should be shared."

I crossed my arms, aware that it only pushed my boobs higher up. "If I kick you in the nuts, it's because you deserve it. There. That's true *and* necessary."

Graves ignored my dig. "So what time is our little gathering?" He couldn't have said it any more condescending if he'd tried.

"As soon as all three of us are at my house. I kinda told her you and I would meet her there since I don't have a car anymore." I flashed him a sarcastic smile as he groaned.

"Okay, fine. I'm going to go inside—by myself—to tell the guys I'm heading out to help you deal with whatever it is you told them you needed me for."

"Shouldn't I come with?" I asked. "Just to sell it?"

"No," he answered quickly. "Because you suck at lying. So once that's done, we're going to head back to my place."

"Your place?" I repeated. "What for?"

The look he gave me was not amused in the slightest; still, he answered. "I might have a solution to your car problem."

Pass the Mic

FOR AS ANNOYING AS MY NEW MENTOR WAS, HE sure had a great ass. As soon as we'd pulled up to his house, he'd jumped out and strode over to a detached white garage to press some kind of hidden button. I'd been a little slower, enjoying the view as I climbed out the passenger side. A girl had to find the silver lining where she could.

I'd just reached his side when one of three garage doors was fully open. Graves' garage was easily the size of a house in its own right. It was more than a garage. It was like an auto shop. Two cars could have fit in the space revealed by the door, but there was only one with a cloth tarp draped over it. In the bay next to it, another car was covered. I could see a part of my wrecked BMW peeking from beneath its shroud.

Before I could say anything, Graves stepped inside and gave the first canvas a tug, revealing a 1967 Chevy Impala. Black, of course.

My breath left me in one low whoosh. I recognized that car. Hell, eighty percent of the population probably did.

But I knew it for a different reason. It was my twin's dream car.

"Shep and I were fixing it up together," Graves said as I moved to stand beside the Impala, my hand hovering over the shiny paint. "We were waiting for a part to come in, and it did right before he died. I installed it right before the funeral. He never got to see her all finished, but . . ." Graves trailed off, clearly uncomfortable.

"I'm glad Shep finally got around to it," I said. "He'd been talking about it since we were kids."

Graves let out a humorless laugh. "Yeah, he was pretty into the idea of being the real-life version of *Supernatural.*"

"Sounds like something he'd say," I said, shaking my head.

"Anyway," Graves said, "the car's yours if you want it."

My answer was immediate. "Hell yeah, I want it." Not only was the car badass, but it would be a way for me to feel close to my twin. Graves couldn't begin to understand how much that meant to me, and I was not about to tell him. Some things were too personal to share.

He moved to the wall and lifted a keyring off a small hook, holding them out to me on one finger. I let my fingers softly trail along the car as I moved around the back and caught a glimpse at the license plate. BAAAAAA.

I stopped dead, a snort escaping. "I cannot believe you allowed him to put that on his license plate."

Graves' lips twitched up in a smile. "You give me too much credit. There was no talking Shep out of anything once his mind was set. You two are a lot alike in some ways."

I narrowed my eyes at the jab. Closing the distance

between us, I snatched the keys from his outstretched finger. "Just try to keep up." I smirked, opening the door and sliding into the driver's seat.

"Uh, Salem? You destroyed one car already, maybe go a little easier on this one?" He quirked a brow.

I rolled my eyes. "See you at my place," I said over my shoulder as I climbed in the car. The smooth leather interior brought me back to better memories I had to keep at bay for the moment. I closed the door and strapped myself in. One twist of the key and the engine roared to life. I allowed myself one second to caress the steering wheel and enjoy the feeling of all that horsepower vibrating around me before I threw her into reverse, only pausing to roll the window down and yell, "Eat my dust!"

I whipped the Impala around and took it easy going down the driveway as the gates opened. Headlights flashed in my rearview just as I turned onto Mansion Lane. It wasn't actually called that, but given that's all that was on the road, it was a fairly accurate name.

I shifted gears then slammed on the gas, taking off like a pro. The car shot forward as I tested the limits. One might think that after being in an accident, I'd take it easy. Thing was, this time I was wearing a seatbelt, and I wasn't searching for Hostess cupcakes—although now that I thought about it I kind of wanted some. I was also on a straight road that led basically nowhere. It was probably the safest place to do this. At least, that's what I told myself.

Truth was, I was a car junkie.

Not for the rebuilding aspect, but for the speed. The power.

Behind the wheel of a sick ride like this, I was on top of

the world, until my own gates came into sight. I realized a second too late that I didn't have the remote control to open the gate.

Stopping out front, I debated the merits of hopping it and decided that ten-foot monstrosity would be a bitch to climb. I was still considering my options when Graves' car rolled up behind me. The giant S filigree split apart as the entrance opened.

That bastard must have had Shep's clicker. As I rolled down the driveway to the Shroud mansion, I made a mental note to steal it out of his car before he left.

My brother and I kept our mother's last name: Kaine. But my father was a Shroud. His ancestors, along with the other founding families like the Graves', created Farrow's Square. There were also the Mortes', the Scythes', and a few other death-like names. In hindsight, I should have realized something was up sooner before it took me dying to find out. But, hindsight was a bitch like that.

I stopped halfway around the circle driveway and hopped out. Tamsin wasn't here just yet, and I suspected it might be a little while given her free rein with my credit card.

Graves stopped behind me and came to join me as I started for the door.

"What are you planning to tell your aunt?" he asked as we approached.

I shrugged. "If I'm lucky I won't even have to explain. She's not all there anyways."

Little did I know how fast my point would be proven.

I opened the front door and standing there in the living room right off the entry was my aunt, Esme.

Naked. Painting a canvas on a standing easel with an oversized palette in her other hand.

My jaw dropped as I tried to find the words.

"Salem," my aunt said happily. She set aside the paint palette and brush, and I saw way more of her than I ever wanted to in that single motion as *everything* up front was now on display. "I'm so happy you decided to come home—"

"Esme, what are you doing?" I asked, folding my arms over my chest uncomfortably. Graves was silent beside me, and I didn't even want to look and see what his face said.

"Painting," she answered, like it was obvious.

"*Without clothes?*" I prompted, trying to see where she thought this was a good idea.

"Well, they get dirty every time," she said. "Even with a smock on I somehow end up with paint everywhere. I figured this way I could just shower off when I'm done."

Well, there was a certain amount of logic there.

I suppose it shouldn't have surprised me. She always was a bit more . . . eclectic in her hobbies. Like my father, she inherited a vast fortune that made it where she didn't need a real job. In lieu of that, she'd taken up some rather interesting hobbies over the years. Tree shaping. Making ASMR YouTube videos. Taxidermy.

You know, the usual stuff.

"Can you just . . . cover yourself or something?" I asked in a pained tone, staring at her forehead.

"Don't be a prude, Salem, dear. The human body is a beautiful thing."

Graves started to laugh but covered it by coughing.

"So that's a no on the clothes, then?"

My aunt lifted her shoulder in a shrug. "I have nothing to be embarrassed about. I don't see why you do."

"Of course you don't," I muttered, grasping Graves' arm and pulling him along behind me. It's hard to forget, but spend enough time away and you eventually do. While a strong woman, Esme was also a bit odd . . . and just a few bolts short of being certifiably cuckoo.

"Nice to see you again, Esme," Graves called over his shoulder as I dragged him out of the foyer and down the hall on the left.

If my aunt replied, I didn't hear it. I was too busy booking it to my room.

"Shep always said your aunt was eccentric, but that's the first time I got—"

"An eyeful?" I supplied.

"Yeah."

Dropping his arm, I opened my door and walked into my old room. It was exactly the way I left it. Band posters lined the walls, a sweater was tossed over the corner of my bed, and a book was open on my desk like I'd stepped out in the middle of reading, which, come to think of it, may have been the case.

"I see the love of 80s music was something you and Shep had in common," Graves said, still standing in the doorway as his eyes scanned the room.

I shrugged and moved to the bed, my hand reaching automatically for the little stuffed sheep Shepard had crocheted for me. It was hideous. A baby blue sheep with little white bones stitched on top of it like a weird suit of armor. Esme had been going through a crochet phase, which was one of her more normal hobbies, and Shep had been eager to learn. The stuffie may be ugly, but it was still impressive, considering.

Setting it back down, I faced Graves once more. "It could have been worse, I guess," I said, returning to our talk about Esme.

"Worse than your aunt being naked?" he asked with a bemused lift of his brow.

"Yeah. She could have been doing her throat singing. Or taxidermy. Or there was that time she was selling sex toys, and kept trying to get me to test them out and give her reviews."

Graves held up his hands, his shoulders shaking with laughter. "Okay, I get it." He laughed a little longer and then looked at me with curious eyes. "So, did you do it?"

"Do what?" I asked.

"Test out her toys?" The sensual curve of his lips as he grinned made my cheeks heat.

"Why, do you need some?" I replied like a smartass, ignoring the way my heart began to beat faster. "I think there's a drawer that still has a few in their packaging. I'm sure if you ask she'd be more than happy to make a personal recommendation for you."

"I'm good, thanks," he said, his lips still twitching with laughter.

"That's what I thought."

"Thought about what?" Tamsin asked, pushing past Graves as she walked into my room, dragging a hot pink suitcase behind her.

Any amusement lingering on Graves' face vanished at the appearance of my best friend. In response, she pulled the suitcase up in a standing position and crossed her arms over her chest.

"Grimm," she said, lips pursed.

"Succubus," he replied in kind.

I groaned. "Are you two seriously going to do this right now?" I asked them both. They looked between each other and me. Tamsin broke first, letting out a frustrated breath.

"I'm sorry; it's just an adjustment. His kind and mine don't get along well. Largely because they like ripping our souls out and shredding them. Kinda hard to find a middle ground when that's the starting point," Tamsin said. Graves' stare only hardened at her words, and I sensed this going downhill quickly.

"You're the one that suggested this meeting, Tam. Hard as it might be, get it together, because I'm a Grimm now too. You need a middle ground? You're looking at it." I motioned to myself and the tension left her shoulders.

Graves sighed. "So where do we start?"

"I think you two need to accept that you're different species, and while you don't like each other, when I'm around you need to at least try to be civil. Sort of. We don't have all of eternity for you two to argue—wait, do we?" I asked. "Is this like books and movies? Do I get to live forever?"

The concept of eternity was entirely new and insanely scary when it was a real possibility.

"No," Graves answered. "It doesn't work that way."

"But that's a great example of why we need to do this," Tamsin followed up, coming to sit next to me on the bed. "You need supernatural 101, so to speak. What you are. What you can do. What you can't do—and why. All that jazz the rest of us learn when we come into our powers." She took my hand and squeezed. The moment was short, but sweet. Then she got up and hauled the suitcase across the room, closing the door as she did so.

"Okay, so, what's first?" I asked.

"The history," Graves said.

At the same time, Tamsin answered, "The Council."

And just like that, we were back to them glaring at each other.

"If we start from the beginning, it's easier to head off her questions," Graves said, defending his position.

"I already gave her the gist of it," Tamsin answered haughtily as she unzipped the suitcase and started unpacking it into the chest of drawers. "You assholes have been killing off my kind and everyone else's for a few hundred years; lately we started fighting back. There. Done."

"That is such an oversimplification it's not even accurate—"

"And your version of the history is?" Tamsin asked, lifting a well-defined brow.

"Alright," I said, cutting them both off as they opened their collective mouths to go at it some more. "Here's what we're going to do." I got up and plucked my old hairbrush off the vanity, extending it toward Graves.

"You're giving me a . . . hairbrush?" he asked, looking from it back up to me. "I'm not sure what this is supposed to do exactly—"

"It's your mic," I answered, pulling out my cell phone. "Each of you gets five minutes. You pass it back and forth and neither of you can talk when the other has the mic. Got it?"

My answer came in the form of disgruntled huffs under their breath. Given what I was working with, I'd take it.

Graves' hand wrapped around the brush, a fire lighting in his eyes as he started. "In order to understand what you are, it's important that you know why reapers exist. The Black Plague wasn't because of a bunch of diseased fleas carried by rats like you were taught in school. It was actually a pack of rogue vampires. In order to reestablish the balance, reapers were created to cull the rogues and keep the peace. Boundaries were drawn, all with the purpose of ensuring humans never found out about our world. When those boundaries are threatened, reapers step in and eliminate the threat. We're actually named for the Brothers Grimm. They were the two most famous reapers," he added when I opened my mouth to ask why. "Their stories have been modified over time, but the originals were retellings of their most infamous supernatural takedowns. "

Tamsin scoffed, and I glared at her. She rolled her eyes and mimed locking her mouth.

"So we're like the police, and the judge and jury?" I asked.

Graves nodded. "Yes, originally. As you can imagine, it's quite hard to kill a supe. Every species has a weakness, but a reaper is the ultimate weapon against all supernatural kind. We were created for this purpose. We are faster, stronger, and more gifted than those we hunt. We have to be. It's how we're able to capture the condemned. Once captured, we remove the soul from the body and shred it to ensure that the creature cannot come back to life and continue breaking the law—which even a succubus can admit would put the entire supernatural community at risk."

"Seems harsh," I muttered.

Tamsin gave me a look that clearly said, "You think?"

"So what happens to a soul once it's shredded?" I ask.

Graves shrugs. "It depends. Most fade away, but sometimes a very powerful being can attach itself to an empty vessel—"

"Attach itself?"

Tamsin coughs, not so subtly saying, "demons," under her breath.

Graves glared at her but did not correct her. "It's what you've heard of as possession or hauntings," he said to me. "Both are caused by shredded souls that have attached themselves to something physical in order to stay anchored to this world."

The phone alarm went off, and Tamsin was already holding out her hand demanding the hairbrush. Graves handed it over, looking like he was far from finished. I reset the timer.

"Okay, go."

"So fast forward a few hundred years. The Council was made to help establish equal representation for all supernatural species. Grimms aren't allowed to just *decide* who gets to be reaped anymore. They did that for so long that many species are on the brink of extinction. Yes, reapers are still the head of the Council, but now there are rules that say what level of punishment is allowed for certain crimes. For more complex cases, the Council has to agree on a reaping. Everyone in Farrow's Square is governed by the Council's laws. In fact, once a supe comes into their power, they need to register with the Council. No one is permitted to leave their town without permission from the Council. It's part of how they ensure that the human world is kept safe from us."

"Are there other Councils?" I asked.

"Outside Farrow's Square?" Tamsin replied.

"Yeah."

"No." She shook her head. "That's why all supes are required to register and stay in Farrow's Square. It's the only supe haven in the world."

"But I left town," I said. She smiled, but it wasn't happy. It was like she knew I was going to say that.

"Yes, because everyone thought you were human. Humans can come and go as they please. But the rest of us have to stay here. Why do you think I never followed you to LA?"

I spluttered for a moment, and she lifted both eyebrows. "I thought you were invested in being a legacy at Grimm University," I said.

"That's because I couldn't tell you otherwise. I wanted to follow you there the whole time, but we don't get to leave. If you register as a Grimm, that's your fate. Whether or not they accept you—which they likely won't because it's been a sausage fest for their entire history." She paused, looking at Graves' face with a sick satisfaction. He clearly wanted to speak, but without the mic he chose to stand there and grimace.

"Why has there never been a girl reaper before?" I asked.

"Because the gene only goes to males," Graves said, interrupting as Tamsin opened her mouth to answer.

"First, it's my turn, reaper. Second, how many women have your brotherhood tried to trigger before?" she asked.

Graves opened and closed his mouth before finally saying, "None. Obviously. The only way to trigger a Grimm is for them to die by supernatural means."

"But I didn't," I said. "I got in a car accident."

"We'll come back to that," Tamsin said. "But first I want to address the obvious. What are the odds that every woman in the original families' lines were actually reapers, just like Salem? What if you guys were just too misogynistic to even consider it, and because of that you think only guys can do the job? Just food for thought." Tamsin was looking pretty damn proud of herself at that moment given Graves didn't have an answer. "Now," she said, turning back to me. "You died in an accident, but you said something ran into the road. What if whatever that was, was supernatural and therefore counted—which is why you transitioned when you died?"

"I suppose," I said, thinking back on it. "I don't remember what it was exactly. Only that it had red eyes and a lot of fur . . ." Which, as soon as you think about it, really only led to one thing.

"Red eyes," Tamsin repeated, looking back and forth between me and Graves. "Sounds supernatural to me." Graves opened his mouth to talk, and Tamsin said, "Don't even think about it."

"But you're guessing based on a single detail," Graves said, clearly exasperated. "Maybe it counted, maybe not. Either way, we don't know if every girl is a reaper. Maybe it's because Shepard died, and they were twins."

She glared at him. "It's possible, but given you guys

have never tested it, I'm not ruling it out. And either way, if she goes before the Council, the only species she can be lumped in with is you guys."

"But I don't want to go before the Council," I said, interrupting her, because unlike them I didn't have to follow my rules. "We know I'm a Grimm. The Council doesn't. And Graves here said a werewolf killed my dad and brother. If I go to the Council, they'll then know what I am, because everyone is represented. Right?"

They nodded.

"Until I catch whoever, or whatever, killed my father and my brother, I don't want to go anywhere near the Council."

Graves opened his mouth, but Tamsin beat him to the punch. "That's easier said than done. If anyone catches you using your powers, they could report you. You'd have to hide what you are from everyone but us. Do you really think you could keep that up for long? You're not exactly the most subtle person in the world."

"If I had to . . ." I started, but she wasn't wrong. As both she and Graves pointed out, I was a shit liar.

"We'll protect you for as long as we can," Graves said, speaking for both of them. Tamsin wasn't thrilled about it, but she nodded alongside him. "Regardless of what you do about the Council, you need to learn how to use your powers. If you get caught unaware, you could out yourself without even knowing it."

"So what does that look like?" I asked Graves, already dreading his answer.

"We start with the basics. Cardio, weightlifting, target practice."

I grumbled, not remotely about this plan.

"Once your powers manifest we'll go into seeing souls and how to remove and shred them. But for now, we'll keep it simple. Tomorrow's leg day."

Tamsin was smirking, knowing exactly how miserable I was at the thought alone.

"I hate both of you," I said, crossing my arms.

Graves shrugged. "I can live with that."

"You should ask them what to do about us," a nasally voice said from behind me. I jumped and spun, my hand over my heart as it thundered in my chest.

"Who the fuck invited you?" I gasped, staring hard at the unfamiliar male. He looked like some kind of Gothic poet, dressed like he was straight out of the eighteen hundreds, complete with lace cuffs and a piece of white fabric wrapped around his throat. His hair was greasy, hanging around his pale face in a limp curtain. His thin lips were pressed together, and his eyes were just as dark and creepy as Not-Morticia's.

"Salem . . . who are you talking to?" Tamsin asked, concern thick in her voice.

I spun around, looking between both of them. "Don't you see him too?" I asked Graves.

His eyes darted to the corner of the room where I'd been staring. "Uh . . . no?"

"Eddie," I asked, turning back to what I now realized was another ghost. "Why can't anyone else see you?"

"Who's Eddie?" he asked.

I groaned. "Not the point, buddy."

The Edgar Allan Poe doppelganger shrugged. "Who am

I to know about what these peasants can or cannot do? I am here for you."

Despite the fact that none of this was remotely funny, I snickered, far too amused that he just referred to Graves as a peasant.

"Okay, next question," I said, facing Graves and Tamsin once more. "Why can I see and talk to ghosts?"

Graves blinked at me while Tamsin's mouth fell open.

"Uh . . . that's not normal," Graves said. "Are you sure they're ghosts that you're talking to?"

"What the hell else would they be?" I said, looking over at Eddie. "This guy just called you peasant."

Graves' brow furrowed, and Tamsin let out a cackle.

"Maybe it's a girl reaper thing?" my best friend suggested. "I mean you weren't all that sure on the car acci-dent. Maybe her powers work a little different than yours."

"I guess it's possible . . ." Graves said, scratching the back of his head.

"Do you think there is a way to talk to Shep?" I asked, the thought making my chest squeeze a little. "I haven't seen his ghost hanging around but maybe if I can find him I could ask who killed him."

Graves and Tamsin's faces both cleared, and they looked at each other, totally in tune for the first time since we started this chat. "Darla," they both said in unison.

"Who's that?" I asked, my brows furrowing.

"A witch," Tamsin said, closing my dresser drawers with a hard thunk. "She loans out spells for a price. Sells magical artifacts. Knows a lot about a lot. She's kind of the oddball in the community because while she's a witch, she doesn't belong to a coven. She just does her own thing."

"She sounds like a smart businesswoman," I mused.

"Something like that," Graves said. "She's best known for her discretion. If you go to Darla, it doesn't leave her shop, so to speak."

"So she's like Vegas. Awesome." I jumped up from the bed and clapped my hands together. "Sounds like she's exactly who we need to be talking to, then. What are we waiting for?"

The Bitter Bean

"God," Tamsin muttered, stumbling out of the backseat. "This is why I don't ride with you."

I rolled my eyes and shoved the Impala keys in my back pocket, making sure the car wasn't locked. We were in the shittiest part of town and locking your car was a great way to get your windows smashed. This area was falling apart; the sidewalks were crumbling and most of the storefront shops were closed. At the very end of the row, a basic white sign reading *The Bitter Bean* hung in front of a door where the black paint was peeling. The windows were tinted dark enough you couldn't see much of anything through them.

Graves opened the door like a gentleman and waited for both Tam and me to enter. I lifted my eyebrows, muttering, "Thanks," as I passed by.

Inside was about as shitty as the outside. The floor was concrete and stained in a way that clearly wasn't intentional. Mismatched chairs surrounded circular end tables. The front counter was a bar of sorts with an espresso machine and other coffee-making instruments, but it was made of plywood from the looks of it and hadn't been wiped down in quite a while. I approached the counter and ran my fingertip along the surface. It came away with a small pile of dust.

"Darla in the back?" Tam asked. The bartender/barista dude dipped his chin in a nod, his expression blank. He wore his hair short in a buzz-cut close enough to his head that I could see most of his scalp. His clothes weren't exactly what I'd call a uniform, and the scar running along his jaw kept me from uttering any of my usual smartass comments.

He grabbed the counter with one hand and flipped it up. The middle panel swung on cheap metal hinges, squeaking loudly. I cringed but followed closely behind Tam as she walked past him and through a curtain of black beaded strands that dangled from the doorway.

On the other side, a curiosity shop of sorts started. Shelves lined the small rectangular room. On them, jewelry and books and small glass vials filled with glowing liquids all caught my attention. Tam kept walking, clearly not as interested in what this Darla person had to offer. A large body bumped into the back of mine, and I stumbled forward.

"What the—"

"Just me," Graves answered, much closer than before. His warm fingers skimmed the small of my back as he stepped around me. The scent of aftershave and spearmint hit me, making me lean closer. Graves didn't seem to notice because he kept walking.

I sighed wistfully and followed after them, approaching yet another counter at the end of the room, though this one was better built. Behind it, a woman dressed in layered skirts and wearing a gauzy shirt turned to me. Her dreadlocks were pulled back in a bun and a colorful swath of fabric was tied around her head in a makeshift headband. Despite her rather bright appearance, the look on her face was stern, if not mildly annoyed.

"What do you need now, Tamsin?"

My best friend's cheeks turned a shade pinker. "I'm not here for me, actually. But thanks for asking," she said with a fake chipper voice. I recognized that tone. Tamsin used it whenever she was in trouble and about to start backpedaling. I called it her "who, me?" tone, because it was sickeningly sweet and insincere. It was usually reserved for her mother or the cops, so who the heck was this woman that she could elicit such a response from my friend with a single question?

Darla's eyes skimmed over Graves, her brows lifting before her eyes landed on me. Interest was shining in the tawny depths, but when she spoke next, her question was aimed at Graves. "What's a reaper doing escorting a succubus?"

"Don't see how that's any of your business, Darla," Graves answered, his voice clipped.

"You're in my shop. Everything's my business."

Tamsin scowled at Graves, resting a hand on his arm as she started speaking. "We are looking for a summoning spell. You see, my best friend's twin just died, and we were hoping we could contact him to find out more about the circumstances of his death. Can you help us?"

"How's the reaper involved?" she asked, tilting her head as she further studied Graves. His face was blank, but I could feel the tension radiating off of him the longer Darla stared.

"He was my best friend," Graves finally said. "I want to avenge his death."

"I have what you need, but it's going to cost you."

"Name your price," Graves gritted out.

Darla's eyes moved back to me, pinning me in place. "Not you, reaper. This one."

"Me?" I asked. Money was no object, but the way she was looking at me, like I was an insect and she was seconds away from lifting the magnifying glass that was going to set me on fire, was really not comforting.

"Yes, Salem Kaine. You."

Alright, she just went from weird as fuck to creeper in all of four words.

Darla grinned, flashing several golden teeth. "Yes, I know who you are."

"Most people do," I replied, not letting it show how she got under my skin. Pulling my phone out of my pocket, I pried open the case and started lifting out a credit card.

"Oh no. I wasn't talking about money."

I lifted my head, unease coiling in my stomach. I knew without anyone having to tell me that whatever payment she was about to demand was going to be something I really didn't want to give. "What do you want, then?" I asked, trying to infuse my voice with my usual irreverence.

Darla leaned closer, her smile widening. "Nothing much. Just a vial of your blood."

I could hear Tamsin's intake of breath while beside me Graves was clenching and unclenching his hands.

"Take mine," he said before I had a chance to wrap my head around the request.

"A tempting offer, reaper, but no. The price has been set. Pay it or don't." She shrugged as if she really didn't care either way.

"Fine," I said, my lip curling up in a snarl. I didn't like being backed into a corner, but we needed this, and for Shep I would give a whole lot more than a little bit of blood. "But if this spell doesn't work, we'll be back."

"You'll be back either way, girl," Darla replied. "But not for the reasons you think."

She knelt down below the counter to grab something, and Tamsin flashed me a warning look. "What do you expect me to do?" I mouthed.

"Use some caution," Graves muttered. I whacked him in the arm even though I got the distinct feeling I was doing some *Little Mermaid* shit right now and this broad was Ursula.

"What exactly can you do with blood?" I asked.

Her head popped up as she moved to stand once more and dropped a book on the counter. Its spine was leather-bound and tied shut with a string. She caressed it once with the long tip of her fake nail before saying, "The options are really limitless."

I didn't find that answer encouraging. Not one bit.

"Why do you want Salem's blood?" Graves asked.

Darla flashed him a condescending smile. "Why, Alexander, I don't see how that's any of your business."

If it weren't my blood they were talking about I would have found her prickly demeanor amusing. As it was, I was pretty sure I was getting turned into a porcupine . . . or something equally stupid. Maybe a frog. That seemed like a witchier thing to do.

"Are you sure there's nothing else we can give you?" Tamsin asked. "If you know who she is, you know she's rich. She can get you pretty much anything you want. Asking for her blood just for a summoning spell seems like a lot, though, even from you." She gave Darla a pointed look and the woman just laughed.

"The girl will do almost anything for this spell, and I have no need for money. My other less interesting clients tend to have plenty of that. Now," she said, turning to directly address me. "For best results perform the spell on the full moon. Because you're not a witch and will likely butcher the Latin, I strongly suggest you take my advice on this."

"Why the full moon?" I asked.

"Because that is when the veil between our worlds is at its thinnest," she said, pointing two fingers and then bringing them close together. "Also, because a witch's magic is strongest then. Even a novice should be able to accomplish a summoning for a relatively new spirit on a full moon."

I pressed my lips together, because I really didn't like the idea of waiting another two weeks to summon Shepard. What other choice did I really have, though?

"Fine," I sighed. I held out my right arm for her to take the blood.

Darla looked from it to my face and started laughing. "My, she is new to all of this. You really should explain more before she gets herself into trouble bargaining with things she doesn't understand," she said. Then she snapped her fingers twice. "Clay!" she called out.

The black beaded strands knocked together as the barista dude from the front poked his head through them. "Yeah?" he asked, sounding bored.

"I need you to take a vial of blood from Ms. Kaine."

"Wait a minute," I said, holding up both hands. "You want Buzzhead to take my blood? That was not part of—"

"New and judgmental," Darla tsked. "You're lucky I can see your future and know you're not a lost cause. Clay here went to nursing school."

Silence spread through the room, and my only response was a soft, "Oh..."

"Oh," Darla repeated. "What did you think I was going to do? Lop your arm off?" She shook her head, clearly amused.

Actually, I'd imagined something more along the lines of a sacrificial dagger and a violent slash along my skin, but I kept that part to myself. No need to go and prove even further how ignorant about this world I still was.

Clay disappeared for a second before returning with a small red box. He went about setting things on the counter while the rest of us stood by in awkward silence watching him. He tied off a rubber string and pulled out a syringe that made me feel a little lightheaded. I wasn't squeamish, but I'd always had a thing about needles. It's why Shep and I never got those matching twin tattoos we'd talked about. As soon as my ass hit the chair and they pulled the tattoo gun out I was back up and out the door.

A part of me was seriously wishing the dagger had been an actual option right now.

"This might sting," Clay said less than a second before jabbing me with the needle.

I bit back a curse and started singing a Madonna song in my head. The pain was fleeting, and my eyes started to wander around the shop as Clay finished collecting my blood. A brief touch at my back had my eyes darting to where Graves stood on my right.

His brows were low, and his blue eyes flashed with something that could have been concern. Given our history thus far, I doubted that's what I was seeing.

"All done," Clay said, stuffing items back in his box before handing Darla a small vial.

"What, no lollipop?" I muttered, rubbing the area above the bandage he'd placed over the injection site. Tamsin snickered and even Graves seemed to have a ghost of a smile on his face.

Darla ignored me, focused instead on my blood. She held it up to the light, her expression unreadable. "This will do nicely." Pocketing the vial, she pushed the book across the counter. "Remember what I said, girl."

"Wait until the full moon. Anything else I should know beforehand?"

"Only the summoner can speak with the spirit summoned."

"Alright, then," I said. That wouldn't be a problem given I could already speak with the dead. The creepy witch didn't need to know that, though.

She tsked again and let go of the book. "See you around, Salem Kaine."

Not if I can help it, I thought while giving her a tight smile and picking up the book. I didn't bother checking to make sure the others were following before I started for the curtain. I was moving fast, more than ready to get out of this place and not paying much attention to where I was going. There was a soft tinkle of bells as I pulled the door to the coffee shop open and walked straight into another patron.

"Oof," I gasped, bouncing back. The book fell from my hands.

"Watch where you're going," an annoyed voice said above me.

My eyes snapped up, about to lay into the ass who thought he was going to put me in my place. I'd had about as much of that as I could tolerate for one day. The words died on my lips as he stared hard behind me.

"Alex, what are you doing here?"

Graves' jaw was tight as he looked from the stranger back to me. "Hey, James. I was just helping Shep's sister take care of a few things."

James looked back at me, his eyes cold. "Here?" he asked.

Graves shrugged, seeming at a loss for the first time since I'd met him.

"We needed to get some uppers," Tamsin said, coming to his rescue. "Everyone is allowed to self-medicate when there's a death in the family."

Something flickered in James' eyes. Maybe sympathy? I wasn't sure. "I suppose that's true."

"James is my brother," Graves finally said, answering a question no one asked.

Looking between the two men, I could barely find the family resemblance. Graves had clearly won the genetic lottery in the family. Where he was tall, chiseled, and insanely handsome, James was utterly plain. His hair was a bland shade of brown, his eyes dishwater blue, his build average. There was nothing notable about him, except perhaps the interest he was currently taking in me.

"Sorry about your brother," he said, bending down to hand me the book I'd dropped. "He was a really nice guy."

Awkwardly, I accepted the book and gave him a tight smile. "Yeah, he was."

At that James nodded in my direction once and then said to Graves, "Dad's been looking for you. There have been some . . . leads on the case." I snorted, and James gave me a funny look. Tamsin grabbed my arm and dragged me out the door.

"Nice meeting you," she called over her shoulder, not out of hearing range but far enough away he wouldn't feel the need to reply.

"You think he's talking about the—"

"Yup," Tamsin answered in a tight voice, dragging me all the way back to the car. A few minutes later, Graves followed us, and he didn't look too happy.

We were barely in the car with the doors shut before he looked over and said, "You suck at keeping anything a secret. If you're not willing to go back to school you need to stay as far away from Grimm University and Gamma Rho as possible—or someone is going to get suspicious."

"What? I know I'm not great at it, but I can't be that . . ." My words dried up at the look on Tamsin's face in my rearview mirror. "Okay, fine. I just hate lying. Besides, he was openly talking about it in front of me."

"Because Grimms have a habit of thinking the rest of us are too dumb to keep up," Tamsin sighed.

Graves turned in his seat. "We do not."

"Yeah, you do," she said. "Seriously, you guys are the worst. It's like mansplaining but for species." She rolled her eyes.

"Either way," Graves said, redirecting the conversation. "You need to stay away from pretty much everyone while you're home."

"Then how do you expect me to find out who killed Shep?" I demanded.

"By waiting two weeks and then summoning his ghost. It's as good of an option as you've got right now. It's not like I can take you werewolf hunting with the other reapers. Everything we do has to be . . . subtle."

I narrowed my eyes.

"Have you met Salem?" Tamsin asked. "She doesn't do subtle. So if that's your grand plan—"

"We don't exactly have a lot of options right now," Graves interrupted. "I'm going to train her in my downtime and hope the Brotherhood doesn't get suspicious. As for you, keep her out of the succubus house, if you can manage that."

"Here we go again with the condescending Grimm attitude," Tamsin sniped.

"I'm not being—"

"Yes, you are," both Tamsin and I said at the same time. He withered under that, settling back into the passenger seat. I stuck the key in the ignition and backed out of the parking lot.

"Look, guys. I'm not great at this, but we have a plan.

Graves and I can train and work on my powers. Tamsin can come see me at my place. I just have to stay out of trouble for the next two weeks until we can summon Shep and find out who killed him. How hard can it be?"

I really should've known better than to ask that question by now.

Long Walks at the Graveyard

"I'm heading out to the—" My words fell silent as I stared at my aunt. "What are you doing?"

She leaned back and regarded me with narrowed eyes. "Tape art," she answered, like it was obvious. I glanced down at our kitchen table. It now resembled Van Gogh's 'Starry Night'.

"Uh huh," I muttered, shaking my head. I walked around the counter and turned on the faucet, filling up my water bottle. Esme was a riddle that would never be solved. I learned long ago not to bother trying.

"Where'd you say you were headed?" Esme asked, only half paying attention as she laid down more strips of tape.

"The graveyard," I said, keeping it short.

"This late at night?" she asked, seemingly nonchalant. I knew better.

"It's only nine, and it's a Monday night. I doubt anyone will be out there."

My aunt looked up at me, pausing with her arms just an inch above the table. "It's not people I'm concerned about."

"Then what is"—understanding flashed through me—"Oh."

She nodded twice, her lips pinched together as she placed a piece of tape and then wiped her hands on the combat pants she wore. I was pretty sure she'd made the pants herself.

"Please be careful. Bring a mace or a baseball bat, just in case. I've already lost two people I love to wild animals out here." Her words came out of concern but were spoken in the same half-interested tone.

"Sure thing," I answered. What was a mace or a baseball bat going to do against a werewolf? It's not like Esme knew that, or what had actually caused those animal attacks. Not that I could tell her anything.

I made a show of going to grab a baseball bat out of the hall closet. Esme muttered something under her breath on my way out. I couldn't quite hear her, but it sounded like it had something to do with my 'skinny arms'. I shook my head and walked out the front door, leaving all thoughts of my eccentric aunt behind me.

It only occurred to me once I hopped into the Impala that I should ask Graves what would stop a werewolf. If I couldn't use my powers yet, then I should have some other kind of defense. I opened my phone and shot off a quick text:

If one were to have a run-in with a werewolf, how would they go about killing it?

I hit the power button and tossed my phone onto the passenger seat as I pulled around the driveway. The Shroud gates split open, and I turned out onto Mansion Lane.

Fun fact: every lot on the street was a mansion. Except

for one. Rather than a home for the living, this one was a resting place for the dead. The graveyard sat between my property and the Morte's residence. I'd run past it the day before while training with Graves. Or, I should say, panted like a mofo, holding my side and watching as Graves ran past it.

Reaper or not, I wasn't cut out for this running shit.

I pulled into the small parking lot and ignored the trickle of unease that ran through me. Of course I was uncomfortable. I was at the cemetery where both my dad and brother were buried. The only member of my immediate family not buried here was my mother. She'd been cremated per the request in her will and scattered into the ocean. It was the main reason Shep and I kept her name. It was all we had left of her.

While I'd been back in town a few days, I'd been avoiding coming here and using the craziness of my newfound reaperness as an excuse. With nothing but downtime now that I was supposed to be keeping a low profile, I didn't really have that excuse anymore. And I was anything if not honest with myself.

While an asshole, self-awareness was kinda my thing.

So here I was. Sitting in an idling Impala staring up the stone path at a sea of ancient headstones. Leaving everything but my phone in the car, I killed the ignition and made my way up the path, walking through the black wrought-iron gate.

As I continued down the main walkway, mausoleums that dated back to the eighteenth century tracked my progress. When I got to the one labeled Shroud, I turned left, not pausing to pay respects to the ancestors within. There was really only one person I was here for.

I slowed to a crawl as I reached the newest grave. The mound of dirt was still fresh and the square, white marble headstone practically shone in the darkness. *Shepard Desmond Shroud. Brother and Friend.* That was it. All that was left to encapsulate the man my brother had been, and it didn't even begin to scratch the surface.

I sank to my knees next to the grave, my hand briefly resting on the headstone beside Shep's. *Hi, Dad,* I thought, knowing I would come back another time for him.

Now that I was here, the grief I'd been avoiding bubbled up. But it wasn't tears threatening to choke me. It was anger. I was so fucking pissed. But not at Shep. Okay, not only at Shep. I was mad at myself; at the way I'd left things between us.

Shepard was the reason I'd run away from Farrow's Square in the first place. We'd had the mother of all fights a few days after our dad died. He wanted to join Gamma Rho, the very people that were with our father and claimed it was an animal attack when it clearly wasn't. I thought he was being an idiot, deciding to join them when obviously something was going on. I didn't realize it was supernatural related or that my dad led a secret life. Maybe my brother did though. Maybe he joined because he didn't have a choice. There were a lot of maybes about why he did what he did, that I never found out because I'd packed my car and left that night. I didn't speak to my twin after that.

"I guess going and getting yourself killed is one way to make sure you got the last word," I said, my voice coming out huskier than usual because of the emotion I was fighting. My hand fisted in the dirt. "But I was right in the end. You did go and get yourself killed, just like Dad. God, Shep. Why? Why weren't you more careful?" I broke off, not wanting to continue down the tangent that had been the reason for our fight in the first place.

"I'm sorry," I said, my voice hoarse. "I'm so fucking sorry. I should have been here—"

The crack of a branch had my head snapping up and around.

"Hello? Is somebody there?" Silence swelled, and I settled back on my heels. *Fuck.* Now I was jumping at shadows because of all this 'monsters are real' stuff. Turning back to my brother's grave, I said, "We're going to need to do something about this headstone. Fix your name. Spray paint it with glitter or something. Hell, even a coat of silver would be more of a fitting tribute than this boring white-bread piece—"

My words cut off once more as the rustle of leaves sounded, closer this time. I froze, the hair on the back of my neck lifting in warning. I pushed to my knees.

"Who's there?" I called out. Dread thickened in my stomach as I slowly got to my feet.

Not even ten fucking minutes and something was going down.

I pulled my phone from my back pocket and swiped up, turning the flashlight on. I positioned it outward, looking over the headstones, but it was all shadows and night.

All of a sudden a person materialized in front of me.

"Not-Morticia?" I asked, dropping my hand to my side as I let out a sigh of relief.

Her expression was anything but.

"Run," she said.

"What?" My muscles froze up as they attempted to turn every which way.

"Run!" she shouted at me, then burst apart in a puff of smoke.

Not needing to be told twice—okay, maybe it was twice—I took off down the row of Shroud tombstones. The pounding of feet on hard earth behind me shook me to my core. It didn't sound like plastic soles slapping the ground. The thudding was hard. Whatever was chasing me was heavy.

I wheeled around a corner, catching a glimpse of my stalker out of the side of my eye.

Large and four-legged, the black-furred creature was hauling ass as it headed for me. I didn't get the greatest look at it, but a certainty filled me as I recognized the single most important feature.

Red eyes.

Did all werewolves have them? Were they specific to this one?

My thoughts raced, trying to find answers that I had no business asking while my life was on the line. I regretted leaving that baseball bat in the car. It may have done nothing more than put something between that thing's teeth and my neck for all of two seconds, but that was two seconds longer than I would have now.

My legs burned and my chest squeezed as I ran as fast as I could through the graveyard and toward the entrance.

The air was knocked from my lungs as something heavy crashed into my side and I went flying.

Pain erupted in my back. Stone cracked. I didn't have to

look to know the damn overgrown dog just threw me into a headstone with a swipe of its paw.

"Motherfucker," I moaned, rolling forward. My knees hit the ground, and I forced myself to stand, to get up, to do something.

Two people in my family died to this thing. I'd be damned if I'd be the third.

"Listen here, you piece of shit," I huffed, pulling my car keys from my pocket. The silver key wasn't likely to do much of anything, given its head was the size of my chest and only five feet from me. I waved the key, slashing it back and forth like a weapon.

The wolf looked between it and me, red eyes narrowing.

My heart dropped into my stomach as the idea of dying —really dying—started to look more and more likely. I was only just beginning to question if I needed to start believing in some reaper god when the strangest thing happened.

A whistle pierced the air and the wolf froze.

Its head turned.

A second sounded from the other end of the graveyard.

And for the first time in my life, an actual goddamn miracle happened. Well, not counting the whole coming back to life thing, which I was still on the fence about.

The wolf turned away and took off in the direction the shrill sound came from. My heart was still pounding, my breath coming to me in shallow gasps as I stared in shock at its retreating back.

My stupid morning runs with Graves were looking a whole lot more important right now. Adrenaline was causing my hands to shake as I shoved my keys back in my pocket and retrieved my phone once more, the thought of Graves reminding me that he should probably know I'd just found the werewolf he'd been hunting.

There were seven texts waiting for me, each one sent less than a few minutes apart. Grimacing, I opened my messages.

> Hard to have a run-in with a Were if you're staying home like you were told.

> You are home, right?

> Salem, where are you right now?

> Goddamnit, Salem. Do you ever listen? Call me back.

> I mean it, Salem. Call me. NOW.

> I'm on my way to your house . . . you better be there.

And then the most recent text, sent less than two minutes ago.

> You are in so much fucking trouble when I find you.

If not for the fact that I'd almost just become a wolf's dinner, I might have been a little worried about his threat. But right now? Getting yelled at by Graves didn't even make the list of things that scared me. He could yell all he wanted, and I would yell right back.

Still breathing heavy, I made my way back to the parking lot, random tremors still working down my body. Headlights bounced down the drive as a familiar blue convertible rolled to a stop. Graves jumped out without turning the car off. He took one look at me and bit off a curse.

"How'd you find me?" I asked, trying to head off his interrogation.

"Esme."

I nodded. He did say he went to my house.

"What the hell happened, Salem? You can't just send me a text like that and then pull a Houdini."

"It wasn't intentional. The werewolf thing. That was a coincidence."

A muscle ticked in his jaw as he stared at me, his chest rising and falling rapidly. I couldn't tell if he was worried or well and truly pissed. Maybe it was a bit of both. It usually was when it came to him.

"Explain," he ordered.

"The part where I wanted what seems like vital information, or the part where I just got chased by a werewolf?"

"You what?" he snapped, jolting like he'd just been touched by a live wire.

I sighed, feeling my body relaxing the longer I stood there in the parking lot. It was almost like it finally realized I was actually safe. But that was crazy, right? It was just this dickhead Graves with me. "I was going stir-crazy at home, so I came to visit Shep. A werewolf came out of the woods and started chasing me. It almost got me too, but someone whistled, and it went off in the other direction. You didn't mention that werewolves could be controlled," I added, accusingly.

"Because they can't. They aren't domesticated animals. You can't make a pet out of them."

I shrugged, knowing what I'd heard and seen. "Well, apparently you can because that's exactly what happened."

Graves shook his head. "You were under attack. It's easy to misread what's going on around you. I'm not saying that's not what you *think* happened—"

"No, Graves. I didn't 'think' anything. That's what happened. Whether you want to believe it or not." I crossed my arms over my chest, staring him down.

"You know what? Why don't we go back to your house and have this conversation there—"

"Hey Graves," a voice from behind me said. I jumped about a foot off the ground, wheeling around and pulling out my little silver key, about to cut a bitch.

"Dom," Graves said, touching a hand to my arm holding the key. I lowered it a fraction, eyeing him and the guy that just stepped out of the woods with more than a little distrust.

Dressed in dark jeans and a leather jacket, the guy standing across the parking lot from us didn't look like a serial killer, but coming out of the woods like that was weird as fuck. Especially when there wasn't another car in the lot. Who the hell was this guy?

"Who's your friend?" Dom asked, stepping closer. His medium brown skin looked darker in the shadows of the moonlight. He wore his hair short, but not quite buzzed like Clay from the Bitter Bean. The expression on his face was stormy. Serious.

"This is Salem," Graves said, stepping forward to stand next to me. He subtly wrapped his fingers around my wrist, forcibly lowering my hand to my side. I glared at him. "Shep's sister."

"I see," he said. "What are you doing with Shep's sister?"

I didn't like the implication in his voice.

"Why are you walking around in the woods outside the graveyard like a creeper?" I piped up, ignoring the warm fingers that squeezed my bare skin.

Dom lifted his eyebrows, his eyes moving from me to Graves. "Just taking a walk," he answered, a shitty lie if I ever heard one. I would know. I was bad at it myself.

"Yeah, well keep on walking, then."

Graves scrubbed a hand down his face as Dom's eyes widened. "Salem," he started slowly. "This is Dominick, the president of Gamma Rho."

That oh-shit feeling you get when the colors red and blue light up in the rearview mirror filled me. I had to do something quick, but backpedaling would just look more suspicious. "I don't care who he is. I came here to talk to my brother, and you were just checking on me when he steps out of the woods like a weirdo and starts interrogating you. It's like ten o'clock at night. What the fuck, dude?"

Judging by the look on Dominick's face, that was not the right thing to say.

"You and your brother don't seem to have much in common," the frat president said dryly.

"Well, given he's dead and I'm not, I'd say so," I snapped. Whatever reply he had been planning to come back with dried up as he opened and then closed his mouth.

"I'll see you back at the house, Graves. I wish I could say it was nice meeting you, Salem, but . . ." he trailed off, the unspoken words somehow more damning. "I'll give you a pass since your brother did recently die," he added as he started to turn away and then called out over his shoulder, "Condolences."

Don't do me any favors, you fucking prick. I was pissed to say the least but then an even bigger thought occurred to me.

He was walking around in the woods where I'd just come from, and he didn't know Graves was here.

Dominick the fuckface just became my public enemy number one and the main suspect for who controlled that werewolf.

"TAM, THE DUDE JUST STROLLED UP OUT OF nowhere," I said, filling my friend in on the prior night's events while stuffing the last of a cupcake in my mouth. I'd made a special trip to the gas station before heading home from the cemetery to load up on Hostess goodies. If ever there was a time to indulge, I think a near-death experience qualified.

I was already unwrapping my second one when she responded, "Do you really think a reaper would be in on it, though? Why would he be killing his brothers?"

"I dunno," I said, speaking around the chocolate cake in my mouth.

"Can you just swallow already and save snack time for when I'm not on the line?" Tamsin griped. "You're worse than the bitches I live with."

I snorted. "Says the girl who's called me, more than once, while a guy is going down on her."

"Fair point," Tamsin conceded. "Carry on."

I snickered even as I rubbed sleep from my eyes. It was

way too early to be awake right now, but Graves insisted we up our training game. "Who knows why Dom is after reapers? Maybe my brother found out something he wasn't supposed to. It makes it even more important that we summon him. I need to know what Shepard knew so that we can take care of this asshat for good."

Tamsin let out a soft exhale. "Salem, he's like head bitch in charge over there, outside of the Council. You don't actually believe you're going to be able to find anything on him, do you? Nothing that will stick anyway."

"Oh, trust me, Tam. By the time I'm done with him, Dom the Fuckface is going to seriously regret ever messing with my family. He may think he knows about the Shrouds, but he's about to get up close and personal with Salem Kaine."

Laughter startled me out of my impromptu moment. And it wasn't just coming from the phone, although Tamsin's cackles were definitely coming through the speaker. My eyes darted to the left where Graves was walking up the drive. He'd heard every damn thing I'd just said.

"Et tu, Brute?" I asked Tamsin. I wasn't surprised Graves would laugh in my face, but I'd thought Tamsin would know me well enough to believe my threat.

"Salem," she laughed. "As soon as you start referring to yourself in the third person, I'm out."

I sighed. "I have to go anyway. The sadist is here."

"Have fun getting sweaty! Oh, and if an opportunity to just bang one out with him presents itself, you should totally take it." The line went dead, and I gaped at my phone before shoving it in the pocket of my hoodie.

Graves was standing just in front of me by that point, and he snatched the uneaten snack out of my hand.

"Hey!"

"You're in training," he said, sending the cupcake flying in the air. "No more cupcakes."

"But-but-I was going to eat that, you asshole," I complained.

"What you're supposed to be doing is running," he said, glowering in my direction as I crossed my arms over my chest. "Not eating your feelings while gossiping with the succubus who lives in a house full of other succubi—all who have advanced hearing, by the way. Awesome oversight on both your parts there." Graves grabbed the hem of his shirt and whipped it off, tossing the material on the porch next to me. My jaw dropped open for more than one reason.

"What crawled up your ass today?" I said, getting to my feet and trying—and failing—to not ogle Graves' body.

"Someone just had to go and run their mouth last night, getting me into some serious trouble with the president. All of this after she left her house and did the exact opposite of lying low like I asked her to."

He turned, and that electric blue gaze seemed to see straight into my soul as I ate up every delectable inch of his perfectly sculpted abs. As my eyes wandered up, I noticed that his entire chest was covered in tattoos. Two scythes spanned the width of it, crossing at the handles. Above them his last name stretched across his pecs. "That a you-thing or a reaper-thing?" I asked, nodding toward his chest.

Graves rolled his eyes but still answered. "Reaper, and

before you ask—yes, Shepard had one. Once a reaper transitions over, they're tattooed to signify the change."

"Weird," I said, twisting my lips. "I am so not getting a tattoo."

"Well luckily for you, if no one knows you exist in the supernatural sense—you won't have to. Why don't you use that as your motivation for staying out of trouble? Because clearly not getting caught by the Council isn't enough."

I blinked, a little taken aback. We joked around a lot. Well, I joked around a lot, and Graves typically took it like a champ. This time, he seemed genuinely pissed. I wasn't sure how I felt about that. "Look, Graves, I'm sorry I got you in trouble with Dom the Fuckface. I'm telling you, though, that guy is shady. He's literally in the woods at the same time as I was attacked, and someone called the werewolf off. What more do I need to prove that he's our guy?"

Graves shook his head, starting in on his stretches. "Reapers are sent out to check the traps regularly, Salem. There were probably a half a dozen of them in the woods when you got chased. Which really, just makes it even worse. That means even when we're looking for it we can't seem to catch the damn thing." He dropped into a runner's stretch, and I came to stand beside him, awkwardly moving my arm around like it was doing much of anything.

"Maybe you can't catch it because it's working with one of you," I said. "Ever think of that?"

"Salem, that's—"

"Brilliant," I said, finishing the sentence for him the way I wanted it to end.

"Ridiculous," he deadpanned, giving me a look. "Grimms and other supes don't work together. Period."

"You and Tamsin are," I pointed out. Not really sure if that was the greatest example.

"That's different, and you know it. Tamsin and I aren't actually working together by choice. We were just thrown together because I was the dumb idiot that happened to find you in the woods that night." A muscle in his jaw ticked, and I pressed my lips together.

"You don't really think that. You know how I know?"

He looked at me. "No. But I'm dying to hear it," he said sarcastically.

"I've been nothing but an asshole to you most of the time we're together. For some reason, though, you've decided not only to put up with me, but my best friend too, even though you guys are like mortal enemies. If you really thought they were so awful, you would have just washed your hands of both of us and turned me into the Council. But you haven't."

I looked at him with a shit-eating grin and the intensity that he had staring back made my skin tingle.

"Let's go running," he said, eventually dropping the conversation. I let it go. For now. "If you're going to make stupid decisions and leave the house, the least I can do is try to make sure you're fast enough to run away."

"You know, I don't really need to be faster. If you're there I just need to trip you and keep walking."

He gave me a glare, and I smiled sweetly like the asshole I was because everything was back to normal. Sort of. At least he wasn't being pouty and throwing my food in the bushes. "You owe me a cupcake, by the way."

Graves rolled his eyes and started jogging in place. "I'll

tell you what. You beat me to the top of the hill, I'll buy you a whole box."

Now that was some motivation. Graves was already off and running by the time I got my legs pumping. It was a struggle not to stare at his ass as it flexed beneath his pants. The material wasn't snug by any means, but it hugged his man curves way better than it had any right to. It wasn't until I stumbled over my own feet that I was able to drag my eyes back up to the horizon.

I was panting hard, hair sticking to my neck and face by the time I caught up with him.

He glanced over at me, his brows lifting. "You're getting faster," he said, not remotely out of breath. "That means we can finally pick up the pace."

"What do you mean 'finally'?" I gasped, my mouth hanging open as Graves jet ahead like some kind of human rocket. My little plan to trip him as a means of escape was looking a hell of a lot less plausible. With as fast as he was moving up the hill, I could be in a car and still may not catch up with him. The guy hadn't been kidding when he said reapers were fast.

I couldn't help but wonder just how much he'd been holding back with me. The thought stoked a fire in me. I didn't want to be babied. Even if I did hate every second of this. I wanted to be able to hold my own, which meant, like it or not, I was getting up that hill.

Sucking in air, I pushed my body forward, pumping my arms and lengthening my stride. The houses became a blur as I moved. By the time I reached Graves, he was already at the top, doing a few more stretches to keep his muscles warm while he waited.

Sweat was dripping down his torso, one specific drop stealing my attention as it ran down the center of his abs.

The sound of a slow golf clap kept my eyes from dropping any lower. Even though they really wanted to.

"Good job. It looks like your power is starting to kick in. We should be able to start extending our routes now."

I groaned. Leave it to him to kill any satisfaction I felt at my achievement. "Do you kick puppies in your spare time?" I grumbled. "Or are you satisfied with being a thief of joy?"

"What are you going on about?" he asked, bending his leg at the knee and grabbing his foot behind him as he stretched his quad.

"You are a thief of joy. You can't let anyone be happy for longer than two point seven seconds before you snatch it away with some dire comment."

He blinked at me. "I didn't realize that's what I was doing. Here I was thinking I was keeping your ass alive."

I glowered in his direction because he wasn't wrong, but I wasn't going to admit it.

"You know, you'd probably be the hottest guy I've ever met if you just didn't speak. I bet you'd get a lot more chicks that way too."

His gaping face as I walked by was the best part of this morning, and that was really saying something given I had eaten cupcakes. I jogged down the hill, using the momentum to keep me running. My legs were Jell-O and wanted to give out. My breath was coming so hard and fast I was partially convinced I'd pass out from too much oxygen—but I wasn't stopping. Not when stopping meant he won. I was going to show his smug face where it was at, even if it killed me a second time.

I passed the graveyard and looped around, the pounding of feet behind me as Graves ate up the pavement started to make me nervous. While soles against concrete and paws against dirt weren't the same, the instinct to run out of a newfound fear still hit me. I used that to push myself harder, making it all the way up the hill without lagging and back down once more. When the Shroud gates came into view, relief filled me. My feet slowed to a stop before filling with lead as I dragged myself toward the driveaway.

Behind me, Graves sprinted down the hill, at a crazy fast speed I could barely follow.

He was breathing harder when he came to a slow walk next to me.

"How did you do that?" he panted.

"Do what?" I grunted, hobbling down the driveaway and mentally cursing my ancestors for putting the house so far back. I needed one of those automated walkways like at the airport to get me from one end to the other.

"Run that fast," he said. "You seriously picked up speed toward the end there. I couldn't keep up."

I blinked, wiping the sweat from my eyes as the salt started to make them sting. "I honestly don't know what you're talking about. I was running the same as before." I shrugged.

"No," he shook his head. "You weren't, but that's okay. I'll figure out what caused it. Fortunately for me, we'll have lots of practice time now that I'm upping our training schedule."

He clapped me on the back, and I let out a huff.

"Do I still get a box of cupcakes?"

Graves let out a barking laugh. "You didn't beat me up the hill."

"But I beat you back to the house *and* I ran the whole time. I think I deserve some cupcakes. Besides, if you're upping the training schedule I'm going to need the calories to keep this rocking bod." I motioned to myself, and Graves snorted.

"You do realize it doesn't work that way, right?"

"What doesn't work that way?" I asked as we approached the house.

"You don't eat a box of cupcakes to stay the same weight—" One look at my face and he stopped talking. "You know what, go grab your keys. I'll buy you a box. One box," he added. "You're not getting this every time, though. And I expect you to push yourself this hard tomorrow, and every day after. Understand?"

"Whatever, Graves," I said nonchalantly, grinning ear to ear when he couldn't see my face anymore.

"And Salem?"

I paused. "What?"

"If you could avoid doing something stupid that almost blows this before the summoning, that would be great."

"If you bought me more cupcakes I'd be too busy eating to get into trouble—"

"Go get your keys," he sighed. "Before I change my mind."

Rabid Stuffie

THE SCENE OUTSIDE MY BROTHER'S WINDOW painted a sinister picture, and it wasn't filling me with warm fuzzies. Especially since I was less than half an hour away from attempting to speak to his ghost. The full moon hung low in the sky and there was a reddish cast, making it appear far too threatening for something that resembled an overripe piece of fruit.

I pushed the curtain the rest of the way open, letting the moonlight stream in to illuminate the makeshift altar behind me. Darla's book had been sadly lacking in detail about what was required to create a witch's altar, but a quick Google search filled in the blanks. At least, that's what I was banking on. It wasn't exactly like I would know the difference between a legit site or a bullshit one.

After comparing about thirty Wiccan pages, I'd settled on a setup that incorporated only the items referenced on all of them. Somehow, I didn't think anyone else used a Versace scarf as the base, but the black and gold silk felt the most witchy out of everything else I'd found still living in teenage Salem's closet.

I was already wincing as I eyed the scarlet pentacle I'd drawn on the center of the scarf in Maneater-red lipstick. I could have used paint, but that would have required potentially alerting Esme, and I didn't want to give my aunt any reason to inspect my handy work. Four unlit candles were set around the pentacle, along with a teacup filled with salt, and another with water. Completing the altar was my "anathema"—AKA the steak knife—and Darla's book.

I hoped it was enough because it was the best I could do.

Now all I could do was wait for the others to get here. Graves had already texted to let me know he was running late. He'd gotten caught up in Gamma Rho business, but he was on his way and would be here soon. Tamsin had run downstairs to grab a lighter for the candles, so for the first time since being home, I was alone in Shepard's room.

Butterflies flooded my belly, although that seemed like far too delicate a comparison for the twisting knots in my stomach. Maybe geese would be a more accurate description. Stress geese.

I didn't like being in here; not without him. Even though he was dead, it felt like a violation. As twins, we shared everything, so our rooms had been our private sanctuaries. We were only ever allowed in by invitation. Being here now, surrounded by the memories of us together, was painful in a way I didn't have words for.

Moving to his bed, I'd lifted the stuffed sheep he'd given me. The ritual called for a personal item, and since it was the only thing I owned that he'd actually touched and created, I couldn't think of anything more appropriate. Lifting it to my chest, I squeezed it, pretending that it was my brother I was hugging. Shep's distinctive chlorine and sunshine scent filled my nose, and I breathed it in, letting myself believe, for one selfish second, that he was there in my arms.

The door crashed open as Tamsin stumbled in, shattering my moment.

"I thought you were grabbing a lighter, not the whole damn kitchen!" I said, dropping the sheep and moving to help her.

"Well, I was, but then Esme started being weird, so I grabbed some other shit to throw her off the trail . . ." Tamsin said, dropping her findings on Shep's bed. I shook my head.

While there was a lighter, she also grabbed two wooden spoons, a can of whipped cream, some chocolate sauce, and a rope—although where she got that I had no fucking clue. I groaned, shaking my head. "Tam, she's going to think we're having an orgy in here."

"We always could, you know," she said with a lift of her shoulder. "I mean, Graves might be a dick, but he's hot. Use the rope to shut him up and—" The words died on her lips with my scowl. "Fine. The lighter," she said, handing it over. I rolled my eyes just as the front door closed once more.

"Graves must be here," I said, poking my head out the door. "We're in Shep's room!" I called.

Heavy boots thudded against the hardwood floor as Graves' dark head appeared down the hall.

My heart jumped in my chest as his blue eyes met mine, but I reminded myself he's here for Shep. Not me.

I flung the door open and stepped back, letting him through. He unzipped his jacket and laid it tentatively on the bed. His eyes fell on the items Tamsin brought up and a dark eyebrow lifted. "I thought we were summoning your brother."

"We are," I replied, avoiding his gaze as I moved to stand beside the altar.

Tamsin came up on one side of me, Graves on the other.

"So how do we do this?" he asked.

I twisted around to grab the stuffed sheep off Shep's bed. "First, we put this in the center of the pentagram." I set the sheep down in the center of my Maneater creation. "Then we cleanse it," I continued, dipping my bare fingers in the bowl of water. I lifted them over the sheep and let the droplets fall. "Next we form a circle . . ." I muttered, picking up the bowl of salt. I used the hand I hadn't just dipped in water and stepped back. Picking up a fistful of salt, I started by Graves and walked around the whole altar, letting a continuous stream of salt pour. I was almost out of salt by the time I came back to Tamsin and stepped within the circle I'd created before closing it.

"This seems kinda Pinteresty..." Graves muttered. "Are you sure this is how it works?"

"Yup," Tamsin said before I could speak. "I've been to a couple of Witches United's coven meetings. They totally do it like this."

I took that as a good sign as I turned back to the altar before me.

"Next I have to say the Latin words while cutting my hand over the sheep. Can one of you hold the book?" I asked. My heart started to beat faster in my chest. Graves wasn't too far off in thinking that this seemed kinda . . . informal. It was the only shot we had, though.

Outside the moon cast a red glow over everything. Graves picked up the book and flipped through it, trying to find the page. I reached over, our fingers brushing as I turned it to the right page. He held it out for me as Tamsin handed over the kitchen knife.

"Are you sure you don't want me to do the cutting for you?" she offered.

"I'm sure," I said, nodding like I was surer than I was.

I lifted my hand over the sheep and pressed the blade of the knife to my skin.

"Skin of my skin. Blood of my blood. I summon thee, from the grave, up above," I said, first in English.

My hand closed around the knife and a stinging sensation burned in my palm as the blade cut deep.

"Cutis mea cutis. Sanguis sanguinis mei. Ego vocare te: De mortis inferno specu super eum," I said next. Darla was right. I didn't even need to understand Latin to know I butchered it to hell.

I squeezed my hand harder as I sliced the knife downward.

The edge came away red.

Crimson welled around my fingers. Droplets fell.

One. Two. Three.

The flicker of the candle lights was the only sound in the room. It wasn't until my lungs started to burn that I realized I was holding my breath. I exhaled slowly, staring hard at the stuffie.

Nothing happened.

"Fu—" I started, shoulders slumping.

"I—" Graves said.

I spun on him. "God help you if you say I told you so right now. I'm still holding a knife."

His lips snapped shut, and he lifted his hands in surrender.

"Salem," Tamsin said softly, resting her hand on my shoulder.

I shook my head, not wanting to hear it. I hadn't realized how badly I wanted this to work until we—until I —failed.

"The blood is never going to come out," I muttered, my frustration tripling at the realization. Leaning over, I reached for the stuffed sheep.

Before I made contact, its mouth opened and it let out a plaintive, "Baaaaaaaaaaaaaa."

I screamed, jumping back and falling into Graves.

"Holy shit," Tamsin breathed as the sheep started walking toward our feet.

Graves' arm was banded tight across my hips, holding my body into his. If I wasn't in the middle of freaking the fuck out, I might have enjoyed being pressed up against him.

"Sh-Shepard?" I whispered, my hand outstretched once more.

"Baaaaaad Salem."

"Bad?" I asked, annoyance swiftly replacing my surprise. "I summoned you back so that I can find out who murdered you and make them pay. How is that bad?"

Even though I was talking to a crocheted sheep, it was like no time at all had passed since I'd spoken with my brother. It had always been like this between us. We were closer than any two people on earth, but we bickered like two old biddies. There was nothing we couldn't fight about.

"Salem goooooo."

I frowned. "Shep, why are you talking like that?"

"What do you mean?" Graves asked, speaking directly into my ear, his voice low and deep. The feel of his breath washing over my neck made me shiver, reminding me I was still leaning against him. More than a little unwillingly, I untangled myself from his hold. Another time, another place—hell, another guy—I might have said fuck it all and explored the feelings unfurling inside of me. But things were complicated enough as it was.

"Salem?" Tamsin pressed.

Remembering the others couldn't hear my twin because they couldn't see or speak to ghosts, I explained. "He's not talking in full sentences. He's bleating at me and calling me bad." I bit my lip, wondering if my botched Latin had kept my brother's spirit from fully returning.

The stuffie continued to move toward us, but he wasn't making much progress as his little legs slipped and slid over the silk scarf. I snickered. He was about as graceful as a baby giraffe with one broken leg.

"Baaaaaa," he bleated again, the sound tugging at my chest.

Taking pity on him, I picked him up and held him at

eye level. The intelligence staring out of those plastic eyes was unnerving. "Shep, can you tell me what you remember about your death?"

"Coooooold. Daaaaaaaark."

"Great, he's defective."

"Defective?" Graves asked. The sheep looked from me to him, and I could have sworn it narrowed its eyes.

"Baaaaaad Salem," it repeated. This time I had a feeling I knew what it was talking about, but I was so not having that conversation.

"Yeah, he's talking like a sheep. Sort of. It's all 'baaaaad Salems'." I pressed my lips together and glared at the stuffie. He was dead and unhelpful. Probably not the thing I should be thinking in that moment, but it was easy to get my priorities mixed up when he was scolding me about Graves.

"Well, you do get in trouble a lot," Tamsin said.

I gave her a look. "So not helping right now."

"What?" she asked innocently. "I'm just saying that it's not inaccurate."

I groaned, looking at the sheep. "Can you tell us who killed you?"

Its big plastic eyes looked sad as it started to shake its little head. "Noooo Salem."

"Can you confirm that you were killed?" I asked it.

Indecision warred in its expression, but then it gave the tiniest of nods.

"He can't tell you who murdered him," a voice behind me said.

I jumped, clutching the sheep to my chest.

"What?" Tamsin asked.

"Are you okay?" Graves followed up.

I turned and peered out of the circle. Standing in front of the red moon was none other than my ghost stalker Not-Morticia. She stood with her hands on her hips and a nonplussed expression.

"What do you mean he can't tell me?" I asked her.

"There are rules. Dead or not. Brother or not. Brought back or not—he has to follow them. The biggest one being that he can't interfere with the living."

The tension left my shoulders as I broke the circle and went straight for her. The candles winked out and the sheep still clutched to my chest let out a muffled, "Baaa."

"You couldn't have fucking told me that two weeks ago?" I asked her.

She rolled her eyes. "You needed the motivation to train. Besides, you have your brother back. In some form, at least." She shrugged, clearly not seeing the issue.

"You have to be fucking kidding me—" I started.

"Keep training. Be careful. I'll be watching," she said with a mischievous wink.

And then she did her favorite thing. Disappeared in a puff of smoke.

"Goddamnit," I muttered, hanging my head.

"Was that another ghost?" Tamsin asked.

"Ugh," I groused. "Yes, that was Not-Morticia." Tamsin lifted a brow at the name. "She never told me her name, but she looks like that kid from the Addams family—"

"Wait, wasn't her name Wed—" Tamsin interjected.

I scowled at the interruption and kept talking over her. "She says Shepard can't tell me who killed him because it 'interferes with the living'."

"Wouldn't it have been helpful to say that before we bothered?" Graves asked.

"You're preaching to the fucking choir," I said, setting Shep the sheep on the bed. "I'm beginning to think the ghosts want something, but no one is saying what. They keep showing up at weird times and disappearing before they really tell me much of anything."

Graves sighed and rubbed the back of his neck. "So let me sum this up. You can see and talk to ghosts, but they won't tell you anything. You summoned your brother's soul back, and he's now possessing a stuffed animal, but he can't tell you anything either."

"Yup," I said, leaning against the dresser and crossing my arms.

"So basically we know nothing."

"Welcome to the club," I told him with a mock-sweet smile. "Feels great to be in the dark, doesn't it?"

"Now, now, children," Tamsin said, her eyes fluttering closed as she inhaled deeply. "As delicious as this weird foreplay game you two play smells, there's no need to get into a pissing match."

Both Graves and I glared at her.

"Baaaaaaa," Shep protested, not appreciating the succubus' comment either.

Tasmin grinned. "What? It's true."

"Stop sniffing us," I said.

She shrugged, not at all apologetic. "Can't help my nature."

I groaned. "So what do we do now?" I asked Graves.

His arms were crossed, and he was staring at the floor, his expression distant. "*We* are not going to do anything.

You're going to stay here and stay out of the way while I go back to the Gamma Rho house and see if there are any new leads on our wolf."

"You know there aren't," I said, more than a little angry he was trying to bench me again. "You guys have been searching for weeks and haven't discovered a damn thing. We can't keep dicking around. Dom could sic his werewolf on someone else."

"How many times do I have to tell you Dom isn't behind this?" Graves said, pinning me with an icy stare.

I took a step toward him. "Just because you don't want to admit your friend might be a murderer doesn't make it untrue."

"And just because you say he is doesn't make it true either," he said, his jaw tight.

"Alright, that's it," Tamsin said, stepping between us with her hands out. Her pupils were blown wide, the black replacing all other color. "Everybody just relax."

The anger seeped out of me before she finished speaking, my body feeling like I'd just swallowed a couple of Xanax. The frost left Graves' eyes, and his jaw slackened. He looked completely stoned.

"I'm calling a timeout," Tamsin said. "This isn't going to get us anywhere. Salem, sweetie, you're still bleeding, so let's go get you cleaned up. Graves, why don't you go home and rub one out. Maybe you'll feel better. We can regroup tomorrow."

There was a flicker in Graves' eye as if his will was trying to reassert itself, but even he wasn't totally immune to Tamsin's succubus mojo. *He's going to make her pay for this later*, I thought in a dreamy haze.

I didn't even have a chance to say goodbye before she dragged me into the bathroom and slammed the door shut behind us, leaving Graves and my brother the stuffed animal alone in the other room.

When Tamsin turned to face me, her eyes were normal once more, but I was still out of it. She shook her head, giving me a small smile. "Sorry about that, but you two are impossible and somebody had to play referee. Now, where do you keep the first-aid kit?"

Ghosted

AFTER THE SIXTH TEXT IN THREE DAYS THAT WENT
unanswered, I slipped my phone in my back pocket and
went into the bathroom to get ready.

"Saaaaalem," Shep the Sheep called out.

I squinted at him, rubbing the sleep from my eyes.
"Don't you ever sleep?" I grumbled, walking across my
room and flipping the bathroom light on.

"Noooo," he answered.

"Huh, guess that makes sense given you're dead and all." The sheep glowered at me from my bed as I began working my fingers through my pink tangles. "What? Too insensitive?"

The stuffie nodded. Fair enough, I suppose.

I flipped the faucet on and splashed my face with cool water, then used the hand towel to wipe it off. Brushing my teeth and changing my clothes, I turned over the last few days in my mind again.

Graves had bounced after the summoning, and I hadn't seen him since. The part that was starting to weird me out was that he wasn't answering his phone. At all. Was he ignoring me? It was possible, but didn't seem likely. Of all the times for him to finally decide to drop off the planet, now didn't make sense.

He was being kinda sketch where the Grimms were concerned, though.

Despite my repeated attempts to make him see that Dom was in cahoots with my brother's killer, he didn't want to believe it.

I walked in my bedroom and shoved my feet in a pair of low boots that just came up over the hem of my skinny jeans. Leaning over, I grabbed my keys and got to my feet.

Maybe Graves was uninterested in catching the real killer, but I'd had enough sitting around. If I couldn't go straight to his door and ask him—I'd do the second-best thing.

"Saaaalem!" Shep called, running across my comforter as fast as he could to catch me. Three-inch stuffed legs didn't really lend themselves to running, and he ended up tripping and rolling over the side of the bed. Shep tumbled to the ground and kept going, landing right at my feet in a sprawl of crocheted limbs.

"I can't take you, dude. Even if I wanted to, the chances of someone seeing you are too high. You need to—"

"Saaaalem," he bleated pitifully.

"Dude, I really shouldn't—"

"SAAAAALEM!" he continued in a shrill screech that tugged at my heartstrings.

I sighed. "You know, even dead, you're a pain in my ass."

But still, I picked him up and shoved him in my purse before heading out the door. I was halfway down the hallway and going straight for the door when something caught my eye. My mouth fell open as Aunt Esme walked around the counter.

"What on earth are you wearing?"

"What?" she asked, looking down at herself. "Oh, this?" She motioned to the monstrosity that was the astronaut suit. "It's my beekeeping suit."

"Beekeeping suit?" I repeated, eyeing the veil meshing around her face and heavy white gloves. "Why do you need a beekeeping suit?"

"To keep bees, of course," Esme replied, completely serious.

I shook my head. "Whatever you say, Auntie," I said, starting for the door again

"I'm off to check in on my hives," she called over her shoulder as she opened one of the French doors to let herself out the back. "There's food in the fridge. The fire extinguisher under the sink is empty, and I keep forgetting to replace it. So, if you start a fire, it's best to call the fire department first and let them handle it instead of worrying about trying to put it out."

"Why's the fire extinguisher empty?" I asked slowly.

My aunt gave me an exaggeratedly slow shrug. "I had a little mishap in the kitchen the other day."

Did I even want to ask what this 'mishap' in the kitchen was?

Nope. No, I did not.

"Alright, Auntie." Esme let herself out without even asking where I was headed off to, and I didn't waste my good luck sticking around waiting for her to realize it.

I was still shaking my head and chuckling under my breath when I reached the Impala. After all the changes in my world these last couple of weeks, my oddball aunt was the one constant. There was something really reassuring about that.

Sliding in, I tossed my bag onto the passenger seat.

"Baa!"

"Oops, sorry," I said, wincing as Shep popped his little stuffed head out of my purse. "Forgot you were in there."

"Biiiiiitch."

I snorted as I turned the car on and started down the driveway. It was really hard to take a cursing stuffed animal seriously. If anything, it only made me want to annoy him more so he'd do it again.

Foreigner was playing on the radio as we made our way down Mansion Lane, and my brother let out an excited bleat that I think was supposed to mean "turn it up," so I did. I drummed my fingers on the steering wheel, singing along under my breath while my brother attempted to do the same.

By the time I parked in the crumbling lot beside the Bitter Bean, my cheeks hurt from biting back a smile. As much as I wanted to laugh at his antics, I didn't think Shep would appreciate me laughing at him. Especially when his singing—and I say that loosely because it was more like one-word exclamations—was in earnest.

"Alright, head down until we're inside." The stuffie pulled his head back down into the darkness of my purse so slowly he looked like he was sinking. "You know, I think I might like you better this way," I teased. "You're far more entertaining."

His muffled insult met my ears, and I was grinning as I walked into the Bitter Bean. The coffee shop was crowded today. There were at least a dozen people scattered through the room, and all of them looked up at me when I walked in. If Graves knew I'd come here without him, he would be pissed. I don't think going to a supernatural hangout was his idea of lying low.

Not that I gave a shit. If he wanted to keep bossing me around, the least he could do was answer a damn text.

Fueled by frustration, I moved to the counter, nodding at Clay.

"Darla in?" I asked.

He nodded, swinging the bar open for me to pass through. "She's been expecting you."

My steps faltered, and tingles worked their way down my spine. *Super.* Not sure how to respond to that little grenade, I pushed through the beaded curtain.

"Salem Kaine," she greeted me before I was more than a few steps in. "You're late."

"How can I be late when I didn't even know I was coming here until about an hour ago?" I asked.

She gave me an enigmatic smile, pushing a few rogue dreadlocks behind her shoulder. "I take it your summoning did not go as planned?"

"My Latin's a bit rusty," I answered with a hard smile.

She laughed. "Ask your questions, Salem. I will do my best to answer them."

Her sudden willingness to be helpful was almost more unnerving than her knowing before I did that I would be coming to see her today.

I walked up to the counter and plonked my purse down. Shep's head popped out and looked from me to Darla.

"Baaaaad Salem."

I facepalmed. "So the summoning worked," I said. "But my brother didn't come back as a ghost or even able to talk in full sentences. He's defective, although cute this way."

Darla looked the stuffie over, not seeming remotely surprised. "I'm not hearing the question in there," she said tepidly.

I barely restrained myself from rolling my eyes. "He can't speak correctly. He's a watered-down version of himself. He didn't come back like the other ghosts, and he doesn't talk like them either. Why is that?"

She didn't take her eyes off the sheep. "You're not going to like the answer."

"I rarely do these days."

She snorted. "Your brother's soul has been shredded."

I blinked hard, my mouth falling open. "Shredded? What the fuck does that mean?" I asked, even though the sick feeling low in my stomach told me I already knew what she was about to say.

Her brown eyes slid from the sheep to me. "The reaper boy has been keeping you in the dark about some things. If you summoned your brother's ghost—which is in essence his soul—you've only summoned a fraction of it because a fraction was all that was found."

Anger that was always simmering within me turned to a boil. If my brother's soul was shredded, that meant a reaper was behind it. My thoughts immediately turned to Dom. *By the time I'm done with you, you're going to wish you were never born, fucker.* Before I could get carried away planning my revenge, I needed to make sure I had all the facts.

"So you're telling me Shep is a demon?" I asked, recalling my conversation with Tamsin and Graves.

Darla nodded. "For now, he is likely close to what you remember. At least in temperament. However, over time, the longer his soul is shredded, the more corrupted he'll be."

I leaned forward, resting my elbows on the thinning veneer. "How do I un-shred it?"

She regarded me for a long moment before replying, "Reapers have the ability to shred a soul, but they cannot put one back together."

I frowned. "Reapers also can't see the dead or talk to them, but I can," I said in a hard voice. "There's gotta be a way."

Darla sighed. "I'm sorry, Salem. If there is a way, I do not know it, and I know a great deal."

I looked around the shop, biting back the fighting words I wanted to sling at her even though it wasn't her fault. Instead of arguing, which was basically my default, I turned the conversation to something that might help me find the answer I needed. "You said Graves was keeping me in the dark with some things. What kind of things?"

Darla smiled, and I got the impression she was enjoying this.

"You're not ready to know just yet," she said cryptically.

"Seriously?" I snapped. "You don't just dangle something like that in front of me and then be like 'mmm actually no'. What the hell, Darla?" I demanded, slapping my palms down on the counter. The wood creaked.

Darla looked from the counter to me, her expression completely unfazed. "You're a smart girl, Salem. You already know he's keeping secrets. You just don't know what. Next time you see him, ask him about the history of Grimms. Ask him *how* they were created. You know their purpose, but not their origin." She turned away to grab a rag and began wiping down the counter.

"Okay," I drawled. "Why can't you just tell me now?"

"Because," she said. "Things need to happen. Things that have not yet come to pass."

I groaned. How much more fucking vague could she get? "You know what? Fine. Play your mind games. I'll get my own answers," I said, turning to leave. I already had an idea just how to do it.

"Be careful, Salem," Darla called after me, almost like she was reading my mind, but I ignored her.

As I stormed out of her shop, my phone was in my hand and my finger was pressing speed dial.

Tamsin answered on the first ring. "Hey girl! Dying of boredom yet?"

"Tam, I need a favor."

ONE THING THEY DON'T SHOW YOU IN THE MOVIES is how much you sweat when you decide to do something illegal. I could hear my heartbeat raging in my ears like a siren, each nerve-racking step making me pause and shift my eyes from side to side to ensure we hadn't been seen.

A soft rustling sent me a foot off the ground as I jumped and then pressed myself as far into Kappa Phi's back wall as I could go.

Tamsin let out a whispered curse. "Salem, we're never even going to make it up to the back door if you don't start walking like a normal person. Skulking about is only going to make it more obvious we're up to no good. It's not exactly like we have the cover of darkness here."

I peeled myself off the wall and sighed. "If you'd let us do this in the middle of the night like I'd suggested, we would have."

She crossed her arms. "It's a frat house, not a bank. What exactly do you hope to accomplish sneaking around in the dark where a bunch of supernatural twatwaffles sleep? Not to mention that there are likely *more* people in the house up and moving around in the wee hours of the morning than any daylight ones."

Okay, so she had a point. It's how she convinced me that two in the afternoon would be a smarter time to break into Gamma Rho than say, two in the morning. But I felt entirely too exposed. More icy rivulets of sweat rolled down my back. I was going to take the world's longest shower after this was done.

"We don't have to do this, you know," she said, voice still whisper-soft.

"Yeah, we do."

Just thinking about what Darla told me was enough to put the steel back in my spine. My brother's soul had been shredded, which meant a reaper was behind his death. One way or the other, I needed to know how deep their betrayal ran. I needed to find proof of Dom's involvement.

His and anyone else's that might be involved.

Tamsin and I crept forward. Well, Tamsin walked like a normal person while I continued with my bad impression of the Scooby gang. I was about as subtle as a neon sign. I clearly wasn't cut out for this shit.

We were just crossing the hedges between the Kappa and Gamma houses when another rustling made me pause. It sounded close. Way too close. I froze, my eyes closing while my brain scrambled for some explanation about why I was taking a casual stroll through some bushes instead of on the sidewalk.

That's when I heard it.

The muffled bleating.

"Oh, hell no," I growled, my neck twisting down to the

small purse I'd brought. I'd wanted to make sure I had my phone and a couple other essentials. You know, a lock-picking set, flashlight, and a screwdriver. It would double as a tool or a shiv. Just in case.

Tamsin had stopped to look back at me. I opened up my bag as I heard a loud, "Baaaaaaaa."

"What are you doing?" I hissed at the little sheep as it tried to climb out of my bag.

"Haaaaaaaalping."

That gave me pause. How exactly did Shep think he could help me with a breaking and entering? "Uhh . . ."

"Salem," Tamsin whisper-shouted. "Are we doing this or not?"

"Coming," I said, pushing his head back in the bag with a finger. "You just stay there." His little mouth quivered like he wanted to protest, but for the moment he seemed willing to obey.

The frat house was oddly silent. I'd sort of expected to hear the chatter of voices or the sound of a TV at least, but there was nothing. The oversized French doors that opened up to the patio and the pool were closed, and the black and silver curtains drawn. Tamsin and I exchanged a look. I started to move to the window, testing the edge to see if it was unlocked. She stopped me with a hand on the arm and a roll of her eyes. Taking two steps away from me, she turned the door and it swung open.

So much for the lock-pick.

"Well if you want to do it the easy way," I muttered, brushing past her and into the house. It wasn't what I expected from a frat house. Instead of beer pong tables and sticky floors, the interior was clean and tastefully decorated in shades of black and silver. It even smelled nice. I'd been prepared for eau de'frat; AKA beer, weed, and vomit. But it smelled good. Like fireplaces and something else. Sandalwood, maybe?

Tamsin trailed my steps as I moved around one of the overstuffed black leather sofas and started making my way to the staircase. If there was anything to be found, it wouldn't be in one of these common rooms. We needed to find the rooms they didn't let visitors see. Specifically, the bedrooms. I knew they'd be upstairs, but I had no clue how many I'd have to go through before I found Dom's.

The bottom stair gave a loud squeak as soon as I put my weight on it, and my body gave another jolt. Now was really not the time to get distracted.

"You stay here and act as a lookout; I'm going to head up and see if I can find his room."

Tamsin's jaw was clenched, and there was a deep furrow between her brows. She gave a tight nod, positioning herself behind a piano that was to the side of the staircase. It would keep her body hidden if anyone walked by.

I moved quickly, but cautiously, testing each stair before allowing my full weight to settle just to make sure there were no more unwanted squeaks. When I got to the top, I was in a hallway with doors on either side and one at the end. All of which were closed.

A plush black carpet ran along the length of the hall, muting my footsteps. I stopped beside the first door to my right and pressed my ear against it. The only thing I could hear was the sound of my heartbeat. Opening the door, I let out a disappointed breath. It was empty. Not even a box for me to dig through.

Closing the door, I stepped back and went on to the door of my left. This time I was greeted by a sea of white sheets. *Did anyone actually live here? Or were these rooms a front just like the frat itself,* I wondered as I lifted up the edge of a sheet and saw an exact replica of the couch downstairs. Further bulky sheet-covered items were scattered around the room, but all they hid were pieces of furniture.

Dust filled the air from all the sheets wafting, and I fought against the urge to sneeze. My eyes watered as the pressure built in my nose. *Don't do it. Don't do it. Don't do it.* The feeling started to fade, and I took a stumbling step forward, right into the corner of the antique desk I'd discovered only moments prior.

"Motherfu–" I cried out, barely clasping my hand over my mouth to contain the outburst as I hunched over in pain. My purse fell from my shoulder, spilling its limited contents on the floor.

"Baaaaa!"

I was still half-blinded by agony, so I didn't immediately notice the tiny body making a beeline toward the door. Blinking back tears, I dropped to my knees and started scrambling to collect the items. The phone and lock-pick hadn't made it far, and I let out an immediate sigh of relief when I saw that my screen wasn't cracked. My flashlight and screwdriver were another matter. The screwdriver was perched beneath an old armchair a few feet away, but the flashlight was still rolling. Scooting forward, I snagged the screwdriver and pushed to my feet to chase down my light source.

My steps forward were more of a limp. I'd hit that desk right on the corner, and there was no question a nasty bruise was already forming. Rubbing the area on my thigh to try to ease some of the ache, I moved slowly, trying not to make any more unnecessary noise. It was a damn miracle no one had heard me.

Flashlight in hand, I shoved it into my reclaimed purse along with other items. "Alright, Shep, time to get back in —" My whisper broke off when my eyes found no trace of my little demon.

You've got to be kidding me. I didn't have time to waste chasing down my wayward sheep. Peeking my head back into the hallway, I watched just as a crocheted tail wiggled through the doorway at the end of the hall.

I blinked in surprise. The door hadn't been open when I got up here, so how had he . . . I realized it didn't really matter how he'd managed to open the door, and I took off down the hall after him.

"Get back here," I hissed. I don't know why I bothered. My twin hadn't listened to me during his human years. Why would he bother in the middle of this grand adventure? I was so going to make him pay for this. Although . . . I wasn't sure what kind of threat would be very effective for a demon.

At the end of the hall, I paused at the barely opened door. My heart was galloping in my chest, but I still didn't hear anything other than my shallow breathing. Using my shoulder, I nudged the door open the rest of the way. I was half-expecting another empty room, but this door was different. It led not to a room, but another staircase. A staircase that ascended into almost complete darkness.

"Little sheep?" I whispered.

Nothing. Frustration merged with the adrenaline inside

of me, pushing me forward into the darkness. *That little fucker better enjoy his field trip because it's going to be his last.*

It was soon hard to make out anything in the darkness, so I fumbled in my purse and pulled out my flashlight. Clicking it on, I swept it across the floor to guide my steps up the stairs. I forced myself to keep moving, all the while yelling at myself for being as stupid as those girls who always die first in horror movies. Especially now that I knew monsters were very real.

I made it up the narrow stairway and found myself facing a lone silver door, my demon twin perched directly in front of it. Like he'd known it was there—which, come to think of it, he probably did.

"There you are, you little bastard." My words were barely more than a whisper, but the sheep turned and bleated at me.

"Saaaaalem goooooo."

It was a little hard to make out the design on the door from my perch on the stairs, but as I moved closer, it came into sharp relief. A Grim Reaper was etched into the panel.

Something touched my leg, and I barely kept myself from screaming. A fearful glance revealed Shep standing on his back two legs, leaning against me. It almost looked like he was trying to push me back, but that was ridiculous. It would be like a piece of dandelion fluff trying to move a boulder.

Crouching down, I grabbed him and pulled him up to eye level. "Don't you *ever* do anything like that again."

"Baaaa."

"How did you even get up here?"

He was nudging me with his head, but I was still

learning how to interpret his movement and wasn't sure if he was apologizing or still trying to get me to leave.

Turns out, it didn't matter. For the first time since entering the frat house, the sound of footsteps reached my ears. There was nowhere to hide and no way to escape notice from the reaper or reapers walking toward me.

Except for the door.

"Fuck it," I muttered, grasping the doorknob that was shaped like a boney fist. I'd just twisted it when a cold, angry voice sounded right behind me.

"Want to tell me what the hell you're doing here?"

Oops

"I . . . UH . . . I WAS"—I SCRAMBLED FOR WORDS AS I shoved the stuffie into my purse—"I was looking for my earring." I dropped to my knees despite being on the stairs and started patting the cheap carpet.

"Salem, you're a terrible liar," Graves said on an exhale.

"Well, maybe it's because lying is bad, and contrary to what my brother thinks, I'm a good Salem," I said, blabbering on from the nervous energy zinging around inside me.

"Get up," he said, motioning with his hand.

I let out a sigh, my shoulders deflating as I climbed back to my feet. "Okay, look—I tried to get ahold of you for days, but you wouldn't even send me a 'new number. Who dis?' to let me know you're tired of me. So I went to Darla to ask her about Shep. Want to know what she told me? She said his soul was shredded. *Shredded*," I repeated for good measure, in case he missed the implication. "I didn't fuck up the summoning. One of your reaper buddies—probably Dom—did it. This just proves I was right to begin with," I said, speaking in a rush to get it all out before he interrupted me.

"Are you done now?" he asked, sounding both more and less annoyed than I'd predicted.

"Is that all you have to say?" I asked, throwing my hands up.

"What do you want me to say?" he replied, anger quickly leaching into his tone. "I lost my phone shortly after the summoning, but things have been *crazy* here. Another kid died three days ago and I've been stuck dealing with that, so excuse me for not having time to drive over and tell you what was up. I was going to come by your place this afternoon, but you couldn't manage to hang tight for three fucking days—"

"Uh uh," I said, shaking my head. "You don't get to spin this on me. We did things your way and you refused to listen to me, only for Darla to tell me I was right to be suspicious to begin with. Look, you may not have had your phone, but it's the twenty-first century. Get on Facebook and send me a message. Ghosting me because you don't wanna talk is a pussy move."

"A pussy move?" Graves repeated. "Salem, someone died three days ago," he said, his voice rising.

"And my brother died a month ago," I snapped back. "Something that only one of us seems to be remembering. I'm trying to catch his killer before he kills more people. Meanwhile you're being obstinate and refusing to see reason—"

"See reason?" he asked, leaning in, our faces were only inches apart. "You're sneaking around in the single worst place for you to fucking be right now. What part of lie low do you not understand?"

We were both breathing heavy. The scent of aftershave and spearmint hit me. I stared at his face, at his eyes, into the depths of blue so deep I half wondered if it was his soul.

Then I kissed him.

It wasn't a tentative kiss or even a gentle one. I pressed my lips to his and grabbed both sides of his face with my hands. My heart beat frantically in my chest as I waited for him to respond.

Just as I started to pull away, a groan slid from his lips and he kissed me back. Strong arms wrapped around my waist, pulling me to him. Our chests hit and passion collided.

He kissed me back without abandon. Despite the lack of practice he claimed he had, the way his tongue slipped between my lips and twined with mine left my legs feeling weak. I clutched him harder, matching him touch for touch, stroke for stroke.

He tried to control every little aspect of my life and yet it seemed the only thing that wanted to listen was my body. Go figure.

We turned, and my back hit the wall. Strong fingers hoisted me up by the waist, and I wrapped my legs around him—having no idea where this was leading but enjoying the ride all the same.

"I still can't stand you," I groaned as he released my mouth to run his lips along my jaw.

"You're such a brat," he whispered, kissing the sensitive skin beneath my ear.

The insult did nothing to cool the heated flame in me as

I moved to wrap my arms around his neck and arched my back.

The creak of a door, however, did.

"What the hell?"

Oops.

Maybe I was a bad Salem.

Graves pulled back, his forehead resting briefly against mine before he gently lowered me to the floor. As I slid down his body, I could feel every inch of his response to our kiss.

A grin stretched across my face.

No, I wasn't bad at all. According to Graves, I was still a good Salem.

Very, very good.

"Dom, you remember Shep's twin," Graves said, turning away from me, his voice surprisingly even despite the rise and fall of his chest.

The smile dropped from my face, and my eyes narrowed as they landed on Gamma Rho's president and my main suspect. He was standing a few stairs away from the top, his arms crossed over his chest, his expression livid.

"You know better than to bring a bitch up here," he said.

"Who you calling a bitch, dickwad?" I asked, taking a step forward.

Graves stopped me with a hand to my stomach. My body was struggling to remember that we weren't still in the middle of grinding on each other up against the wall because the warmth of his hand sent a flood of liquid heat spiraling through me.

Before Graves could respond, Dom spoke again. "I

thought you were searching for the intruder . . ." he trailed off, his eyes flinty. "Unless you already found her."

I was pretty sure my lost earring excuse wasn't going to do me any favors here, so for once I remained silent, letting Graves answer.

"Cool the hostility, Dom. This is Shep's sister you're talking to. Salem was in my room when the wards were crossed," Graves said smoothly, simultaneously impressing me and concerning me once again with his ability to lie. "I told her to stay put, but she got nervous and ran up here not realizing there weren't any windows for her to climb out of."

A muscle ticked in Dom's jaw. It didn't take a genius to realize he wasn't buying it. "Shep's sister? In your room? Right. You've been acting strange ever since she showed up and you expect me to believe there's not more going on here? Everyone knows she's paranoid. She tried to get the whole place shut down a few years back when her old man died."

Graves shrugged. "It's the truth. She has no reason to break in."

Dom's gaze drifted back to me, and he shook his head. "Doesn't matter what I think. Rules are rules. Any non-brothers found on the premises when a ward is broken have to be taken before the Council for interrogation."

"Dom—" Graves protested. The thread of panic I detected in his voice kept me silent. The last thing I wanted to do was have to deal with the Council.

"No way, brother. I'm not about to break the rules for your fuck buddy. Especially not with everything going on."

"Pres, you up there?" another voice called from below.

"Yeah," Dom said, not looking away from Graves and me.

"We caught her. It was a succubus. She was trying to charm James into letting her go when we found her."

My eyes shut briefly. *Fuck. Tamsin*

His thick brows lifted at that. "Well, would you look at that. Either you two were telling the truth, or your girlfriend has a partner."

Graves didn't betray me, not even with a flicker of his eyes, but I could tell he was pissed. I just didn't know if it was with me, or the reaper shooting daggers at us with his eyes.

"Aw, come on," Tamsin's voice drifted up the stairs. "I can think of *much* better things we could be doing with those hands . . ." I could just see her batting her eyelashes, playing the role of vixen like that would get her out of trouble with reapers of all people. I rolled my eyes and snorted. And they thought I was the problem?

Graves turned and gave me a look, taking my hand to haul me down the stairs. I tugged back, not about to leave my purse—or Shep—behind. Bag in hand, I followed Graves. Dom stepped aside, clear distaste on his face when I walked past.

Given we were already caught, I didn't resist the urge to flip him off.

He let out a huff as I turned my head, using my middle finger to pretend I was putting on some of my Maneater lipstick before mouthing, "Fuck you."

"Salem," Graves said. I turned, blinking my eyes innocently even though he totally just saw that. "Please go wait in my car."

"What?" I asked, looking back and forth between Dom and Graves. "Why?" I demanded.

"I have to bring you before the Council. Please just get in the damn car," he said quietly, trying not to elicit an argument.

"I'm not leaving Tam to ride with them," I said. "I don't trust them."

Graves' jaw clenched. He didn't like it, but I think he knew I was right not to trust them.

"The succubus will be unharmed," Dom said in a brisk tone.

"Your face won't be if you lay a hand on her," I snapped back.

"Salem," Graves groaned—and not in the good way. "Get in the fucking car before you make this worse for everyone."

I pressed my lips together, eyeing Dom with hatred.

"If it makes you feel better, I'll be riding with you instead of her," Dom said, clearly not trying to make me feel better.

"I got this," Graves said. "You don't need to—"

"Actually, I do. I'm not giving you two time alone to get your story straight before the Council questions her."

I swallowed hard, and I think he saw because the bastard grinned.

"You clearly don't know Salem if you think she can lie," Graves said, already defeated.

"Well, we'll find out. Won't we?" Dom said, moving to stand beside me in the hall. He motioned to the staircase that led down to the first floor where Tamsin was standing. She stood at the bottom of it, staring up at me with solidarity. Behind her was the lumberjack from my first time here. He was holding her arms behind her back. Relatively speaking, she seemed unhurt.

"He drives a Corvette. You won't fit, so find another ride," I snapped.

"Lucky for us, he has many cars, and the Corvette isn't here today," Dom said with a smirk. "After you."

"Oh, go choke on a dildo," I muttered, brushing him off.

No one laughed.

Sexy Lies

I GLARED AT HIM IN THE REARVIEW OF GRAVES' '67 Chevelle Malibu, trying hard not to kick the purse at my feet as I crossed my legs.

Dom the Fuckface glared in return from the backseat.

While his mocha skin and regal bone structure made him attractive to an unbiased party, all I saw when I looked at him was my brother's killer and everything that was wrong with the Grimms.

"You're awfully hostile for a girl who's supposed to just be fucking him," Dom commented.

Graves' hands tightened on the steering wheel, his knuckles going white. His full lips pressed into a thin line, but his eyes stayed on the road.

"Maybe because the first time we met, you were slinking around outside the cemetery, a place I had every right to be, might I add," I replied. "And then you had the bright idea to be a dick to someone grieving," I added.

Something crossed his face, almost like regret. It was

gone in an instant as the car came to a halt. I turned my eyes from the mirror to the building before me.

Town Hall.

How . . . basic.

I don't know why, but when you hear about some infamous supernatural council, the meeting place doesn't exactly scream Town Hall. More like hidden basement beneath the university houses with fingerprint access pads and spelled booby traps.

This was downright boring by comparison, but the familiarity of it settled some of the knots in my stomach and the panic that had been slowly starting to creep up on me.

"Time to see what you know, Kaine," Dom said, the backdoor slamming shut as he got out. I took a deep breath and followed. On the other side of the half-empty lot, an SUV was parked. Lumberjack got out first, and Tamsin followed, arms still behind her back in a way that didn't look comfortable. She gave me a weak smile that I knew was meant to reassure me more than anything. I gave her one back, and then the lumberjack shoved her shoulder.

"Get walking," he said.

"Hey!" I snapped, "She's half your size, dickhead—"

"Salem," Graves said in warning.

"Don't Salem me," I said, flashing him a hard look. "Who the fuck put him in charge where he treats her like some kind of convict?"

"Because she is," Lumberjack muttered under his breath. My fists tightened, and I started for him, wishing we'd taken my car so I could grab the bat out of it and beat his ass.

A hand grabbed my forearm.

I wheeled around, ready to swing if it was Dom.

Much to my disappointment, it wasn't.

"You need to calm down," Graves whispered in my ear. His cool breath fanned against my flushed skin. I shivered, and Tamsin let out a whoop despite the hands holding her back.

"Get it, girl," she called out, throwing her head back in a laugh as she was urged forward.

I turned my head a fraction to meet his eyes. "They're not treating her right."

What I saw shining back at me was understanding. "No, they're not. But they won't seriously hurt her before she's brought to the Council. Her mom's on it. They're just throwing their weight around because they want to see how much you know."

I opened and closed my mouth. "Oh."

"Yeah, so chill. In fact, if you can avoid talking as much as possible that would probably be best right now."

I glared at him, mouth opening to hurl another comeback, but I snapped it closed at the pointed lift of his brows.

Graves gave my arm another squeeze, the warmth of his touch seeping through me and reminding me that even though I was about to be surrounded by a room of potential enemies, I was not alone.

We moved up the steps and through the surprisingly empty lobby. It was still late afternoon. There should have been people milling about, but our footsteps were the only ones echoing through the building. Our small group strode past a couple of elevators, moving instead to the back corner of the main lobby.

The door we were heading toward read "Restricted Access" but was otherwise unremarkable. At least it was until Dom's hand curled around the doorknob.

Electric energy arced down my skin, and it was a struggle not to move away from it. Beside me Tamsin let out a low moan, her discomfort looking like it bordered on pain.

My eyes snapped to Graves over my shoulder. "What the hell?" I mouthed.

"Ward," he answered, breathing it into my ear.

Apparently this place just looked basic. Good to know.

Dom led us down a hallway, my eyes trained on one flickering light at the far end of the hall. In every horror movie I'd ever watched, there was always that one struggling light acting as some kind of symbolic warning of what was coming. Almost as if it were the last beacon in the darkness, or whatever.

I snorted as my imagination ran wild with the scenarios of what was about to happen, each version more absurd than the last.

The reality was slightly less colorful.

Dom knocked on a door about halfway down the hall, opening it before there was any kind of response from inside. We filed into a sort of amphitheater, one curved table set out on the stage, seven people spread out along its length, staring at us with completely unreadable expressions.

I recognized Tamsin's mom sitting to the left of a man with Graves' startling blue eyes. Even her expression was frosty, her golden eyes trained on her daughter as her lips curled down in disappointment. Tamsin wilted a little, some of her defiance draining out of her as she dropped her eyes down to the floor.

If anything, that only fueled my own resolve. I would not give these assholes that kind of power over me.

"Well, Dominick, why don't you tell us why we're here," the man I could only assume was Graves' father said, his voice a cultured drawl. It would have been soothing under any other circumstance, but the softness with which he spoke only seemed to underscore the depth of his power.

"As per the bylaws of our house, whenever a ward has been triggered, all non-members must come before the Council for questioning." Dom gave his report like a soldier reporting to his commanding officers. His feet were spread shoulder width apart, his hands clasped behind his back. He spoke clearly, not mincing words as he made references to specific rules that we'd apparently broken. Finally, he finished with, "We caught these two sneaking around after such an incident."

"I see," Graves' father said, eyeing Tamsin and me with more interest. "And do you two have anything to say for yourselves before we begin?"

"I was just waiting on Salem and Graves to finish up so we could go grab coffee," Tamsin said with a straight face.

I swallowed. *Aw hell.* Were we really using fucking as the cover-up? I wasn't even getting some.

"Finish what?" Graves' father asked. His blue eyes flicking between Graves and me. The former took a step to the side, further away from me, and it was my turn to wither a little.

Well. If it's going to be like that . . .

"What do you think?" Tamsin asked with a delicate lift of her eyebrows.

Her mother's lips twisted in amusement. "You're saying they were having sex."

She didn't ask it like a question, but Tamsin chose to answer it as one. "Yes, ma'am."

"And you were waiting for them to . . . finish?" her mother asked.

Tamsin nodded.

"We found her at the bottom of the stairs," lumberjack reaper interjected, his big meaty face set in a scowl.

All members of the Council eyed her again.

"They were getting it on," Tamsin said. "I got a little curious since they were taking so long. I wanted to see if they might like a third . . ."

Oh my God. She did not just—yes, she did.

And her mom was now smiling.

What the fuck?

I couldn't lie for shit, so I really hoped my face didn't betray me right now because I was in next-level shock.

"Interesting story," Dom said, stepping forward. I didn't notice until now that he wore casual clothes, but casual in the rich person sense. Instead of a three-piece suit, it was a button down and slacks. He fit right in with the Council as he started to slowly stroll as if drumming up to tell quite the story. "I'd almost believe it, had I not found Salem Kaine and Graves in the hallway near the upper level of the Grimm house. Graves claimed they were also in his room, that he came to check the ward, and Salem ventured out to look for him."

Well, it could have been worse. I think.

The Council looked to me.

"Is this true?" another member asked, one that I didn't know who or what they were. Although, she did resemble Not-Morticia a bit. With her tight black dress, just long enough on the skirt to be classy, long sable hair, and red lips —she could have been her mother. At least as far as ensemble was concerned.

I swallowed, mouth dry. "Yes."

Stick to one-word answers. Harder to get caught in a lie.

"What made you think that he was on the upper floor?" Graves' father asked.

"I don't know." I shrugged. "Just a guess . . ."

"A guess," the man repeated. I wish I knew his name right about now. "Do you know why you're here"—his attention flicked to Dom—"Salem, you said?"

Dom nodded.

I froze. "I . . . um . . . well, I thought it was kind of weird how they were all freaking out about some alarm I couldn't hear or see. Now I'm in trouble with the city council, and that's really weird . . ." I said, fumbling over my words. "I mean, why would I be in trouble for walking around? And why do Tamsin and I have to explain? It's a frat house and, uh, I was just there to hook up. Getting it on like Donkey Kong, you know?"

"I can't tell if she's lying or just nervous," the lady in black said with an exasperated sigh. "Sarah, just compel them. If she knows nothing, we wipe her memory, making her forget this ever happened and move on. I'm going to miss my four o'clock feeding at this rate."

I swallowed again, for more than one reason.

One, this broad was a vampire. I was face-to-face with a

vampire, and she looked nothing like the ones from *Twilight*.

Two, this was fixing to get a whole lot messier.

"What—wait a minute—what's this compelling thing mean?" I asked, not faking the quaver that entered my voice.

If they started messing around in my mind, my secret was going to get out. I didn't know much of anything of this supernatural stuff, but I was certain that wasn't going to be something I could hide from them.

Tamsin's mother stood and gracefully made her way down the stage and over to us. She paused directly in front of me, giving me a friendly smile. Then she leaned forward and sniffed me, her pupils dilating as she leaned back. "She's telling the truth," Tamsin's mom declared. "I can smell his lust all over her. Sadly, it seems they were interrupted before they reached climax. How tragic."

I could feel the blood rush to my face. It was one thing to get caught dry humping Graves and another thing to have to talk about in front of his dad and frat brothers. I risked a glance at him, annoyed that he looked entirely unfazed.

Seriously? Am I the only one suffering here?

Huffing, I rolled my eyes. "If somebody knew more about female anatomy it might not have taken so long."

Snickers filled the room as Graves tensed, his eyes shooting daggers at me as he finally looked my way.

I lifted my shoulder in the tiniest shrug. There. Now we were both humiliated.

"I'm sorry to hear that my son disappointed you,"

Daddy Graves said, barely hiding his own smile. "Dominick, it seems this was all a misunderstanding."

Dom's face could have been carved from stone. "Sir, I must respectfully disagree. Only a powerful supernatural could have set off those wards. And it wasn't until this one," he gestured to me, "reached the third floor that the second ward was triggered. Their story doesn't add up, sir. Not timing wise, and not with where they were located when we found them mere minutes afterwards. I think there's something else at play here."

"If the girl was a supernatural, she would have been registered. The Council has no records of Salem Kaine, outside of her birth and relation to Shepard Kaine." Graves' father turned to look at a burly man with a scar running down the length of his face and bushy gray hair. "Have any of your pack bitten a human recently?"

"No, Alexander," the man replied in a gravelly voice. "Any human attacks must be reported within twenty-four hours of occurring to ensure that none have been turned."

He was Alexander too? I wondered, confused until I remembered Graves had mentioned he was a "third," meaning he shared his father's exact name. That had to get confusing growing up. How did they ever know which one was being spoken to?

Even though they were talking about me, it was hard to get myself to pay attention.

"Desdamona?" Graves' father asked, turning to the vampire.

"No. We have not turned a human in almost five years."

He nodded, as if he'd expected the answer. "Then I suppose we must call upon your services, Yasha."

My eyes turned to the woman on the far right of the table. She was lovely, in that timeless plastic surgery kind of way. Her silver hair was braided and hung down her back as she stood and made her way down the stage.

"What are you doing?" I asked, glancing sideways at Graves and Tamsin. Graves' jaw was clenched. The muscle ticked. He watched with hard eyes as Yasha came to stand before me. Next to him Tamsin looked troubled.

Yasha must not have deemed me worth answering because she reached forward and grabbed my hand. Her fingers were cold as she turned mine over.

"Hey! I asked what you were—" Using her free hand, she jabbed one of her pointed nails into my palm.

Blood welled in the shape of a half moon. She lifted her nail, now coated with it.

I watched in trepidation as she leaned forward. I half expected her to lick it at this point, but she did something even weirder. She muttered a rush of words I didn't understand and the blood on her finger ran black.

Yasha's eyebrows drew together. She looked confused as she turned and presented her now blackened nail. The Council members faces turned stricken.

"That's impossible," Alexander said.

"The blood does not lie," Yasha replied softly.

"Perhaps the spell—"

"There is nothing wrong with the spell," she said with a bite.

"Here," Desdamona said, waving her hand toward her. "Let me taste it. I can tell you if the girl is what she seems."

Alexander didn't look happy with this plan of action, and not gonna lie, I wasn't thrilled by it either. However, if it kept them from having Yasha jab me again, I wasn't going to say shit.

Yasha walked up the platform and next to me Tamsin's mom looked between the witch and I, worry filling her expression. Was she worried for me? Or about their secret? Or was it because they were fixing to know I was a freak of nature?

I still wasn't sure when Yasha extended her hand. Desdamona grasped her wrist and brought the other woman's finger to her mouth. She licked it gingerly.

Her eyes flared wide.

"The blood does not lie," Desdamona repeated, clearly shaken.

"It cannot be," Alexander said, trying to remain staunch in his opinions, though it was clear they were beginning to wane. "We've never had a female."

"Well you do now," Yasha said, taking her seat.

All eyes were on me as Tamsin's mom, Sarah said, "Salem, did you know that you're a reaper?"

There was an odd tone to her voice. The world seemed brighter for a moment. The air fresher. Beyond it, something I couldn't name touched me. Making me speak. I couldn't stop myself, even if I wanted to.

"Yes."

Blood Rite

THE ROOM ERUPTED AROUND ME, BUT I WAS focused only on the woman standing before me, still ensnared by her compulsion. Until Sarah saw fit to let me go, her will was mine.

"Sarah, ask the girl how she died," Desdamona instructed, peering at me intently. After a confirming nod from Alexander, she complied.

"Salem, how did you die?" Tamsin's mom asked in the same odd tone.

"Car accident."

Brows furrowed; Sarah pressed. "What caused it?"

"A werewolf."

The werewolves grizzled representative frowned. "No one in my pack reported any such activity."

"Lies are impossible under the compulsion," Sarah reminded him.

"You will investigate this breach," Alexander said to the alpha wolf who merely nodded his agreement. "Continue, Sarah."

With a nod, she turned her eyes back on me. "Salem, how long have you known what you are?"

"A few weeks."

Another explosion of whispers and outrage.

"Who else knows what you are?"

I didn't want to answer. To betray the two people who have tried so hard to keep me and my secret safe, but I was utterly useless against the succubus' compulsion.

"I did," Graves answered, shocking the hell out of me and everyone else in the room. "I found her right after she turned. I was the one who told her to keep it to herself for now. Since I wasn't sure it were even possible for a female to become a reaper, I have been waiting for her powers to fully manifest before bringing her to you. I did not want to cause chaos until I knew for sure."

He said all of it matter-of-factly, as if he had not just admitted to what I was certain was supernatural high treason. He willingly broke a law—probably several—by keeping my secret.

The dull roar of voices faded as Alexander regarded his son. "That was not your call to make."

Graves nodded. "I know, but I did what I thought was best. I will not apologize for doing as you taught me."

Alexander's eyes narrowed. "As your father, I can appreciate you standing by your convictions. As the head of the Council, I cannot stand by and allow you to flagrantly defy our laws. It is up to the Council to decide what is best for all supernaturals. Not you. You should have come to us immediately."

Graves dipped his chin in the barest hint of a nod. "Yes,

sir. I will accept whatever punishment you see fit for my behavior."

Aw hell. He was going to martyr himself for me. I couldn't let Graves throw himself under the bus like that. Unfortunately, Sarah still had me bound. Until she released me, there was nothing I could do to stop this train wreck from happening.

Ice crawled down my spine as voices rose up once more.

"The only punishment I'll accept is a public lashing," the werewolf replied.

"That's barbaric," a member said, speaking for the first time. She had jewel-green eyes and dark blue hair. From her back, two beautiful butterfly-like wings protruded. "Violence is not the answer. He should be re-educated in the ways of the Council and stripped of his status as a reaper."

"No, we should put him to work in the diamond mines," a small but well-muscled man interjected. "A few years of hard labor should help drive the point home."

"Or I can compel him to act as a servant of the Council," Sarah said. "That way we can ensure he cannot defy us again."

Alexander lifted a hand, staying the voices. "The laws are clear as to—"

"Sir, if I may?" Dom said, stepping forward.

"What is it, Dominick?"

"What if we invoke a blood rite?"

Instead of more whispers, absolute silence filled the amphitheater.

"Go on," Alexander said.

"If the girl is a reaper, she will need to be tested. It is up to the head of the newly turned to oversee her training. What better punishment could there be than tying your son's fate to hers? After all, he is next in line, and he saw fit to take the girl under his wing and hide her. So let him remain chained to her. Any mistakes she makes will be his; her failures as well."

My breath caught in my chest. As far as punishments went, Graves seemed to be getting off easy. Force us to work together? Fine. We were already doing that. But my self-appointed mentor looked far less pleased about this suggestion. In fact, he looked like he was about to throw up. Apparently there was something more to this blood rite thing.

"If you invoke a blood rite, Salem and I will be tied together for more than just her failures," Graves said. "It binds us in more ways than one. If I am hurt, she will be hurt. If she dies, I die."

"Precisely," Dom said. "Perhaps you'll take your job as a reaper more seriously when your fuck buddy is on the line."

"Dominick," Alexander said sharply. "You're president of the frat. Not the brotherhood. Mind your station." Despite being more than a little worried about the prospect of this blood rite, I did a little happy dance in my head that Dom the Fuckface got his ass chewed out.

"All I am saying is that it is a punishment befitting of what they've done," Dom said without inflection.

"Salem didn't even know about this world a few weeks ago, or its laws," Tamsin argued, piping up from the side. "Don't you think it's a little unjust to bestow this mega punishment on her when she doesn't even get what being a reaper really means?"

The Council exchanged glances, and Sarah took that as a sign to continue.

"Salem, what is a reaper?" she asked, compelling the words forward.

"The supernatural police," I said, seeming to please them. However, since she'd asked me an open-ended question I was allowed to speak more and elaborate. Temporarily relieving me from the forced vow of silence until spoken to. "They hunt down other supernaturals for minor crimes and rip their souls apart. Because of that the other supes are getting tired of their tyrannical ways and—"

"That's enough, dear," Sarah Cunningham said quickly. I got the feeling she was stopping me more for my sake than anything. One quick look at Alexander told me he was not happy with my outburst.

"Is this seriously what you've been teaching the girl?" His knuckles were white as he clenched his fists, staring at his son with condemnation. "If you dislike our ways so much, perhaps you are not worthy of inheriting my title."

Graves sighed, struggling to find an answer.

"Hold up now," Tamsin said, her cheeks a little reddened. "Salem never said Graves was the one who told her this."

"Who told you this?" her mom asked me.

Like the puppet I was, unable to lie, I answered. "Tamsin did."

"You also knew about this, succubus?" Alexander asked, his voice whisper-soft but ten-times scarier because of it.

"I did."

Internally I groaned. *Mayday. Mayday.* This ship was sinking fast, and we were all going down with it.

"And yet you, too, did not see fit to share with the Council?" he asked.

"Salem is like a sister to me. I only wanted to protect her."

Alexander drew in a long breath, his eyes dropping to the table in front of him as he considered her words. "Be that as it may, you partook in a deception against the Council, and as such you also will share in the punishment."

Tamsin paled, but did not argue.

He then looked around the room, speaking slowly but clearly. "I am ready to deliver my verdict. Tamsin Cunningham, while the part you played was minor by comparison, you are far from innocent. You will spend the next month transcribing Farrow's Square's civil and criminal archives. Perhaps time spent reading our oldest laws will help you remember them in the future."

Tamsin gave a small nod, looking solemn but relieved.

"Salem Kaine, since you are mostly ignorant of our laws, that must be taken into consideration. From this day forth, you are bound by the laws of the Council and will be trained in the ways of your species. Due to your transgression, you will be under strict observation until you complete your training and you're on a one-year probation after your testing."

Dom opened his mouth like he was about to protest, but a sharp glance from Alexander stemmed the words.

"Alexander, as my heir, you above all others should understand the importance of the Council and the stupidity of your actions. Your betrayal cannot be overlooked. I invoke the blood rite to be performed immediately. From this moment on, your fate is tied to Ms. Kaine's. Teach her well; your lives depend on it."

Tamsin sucked in a sharp breath while Dom was openly grinning at us. The rest of the Council seemed satisfied with these punishments, despite their earlier suggestions.

With an apologetic smile, Sarah finally released me from her compulsion. "This will all be over soon," she murmured.

"But you just said I would get a lighter punishment," I argued. "I'm still getting the same thing as Graves and you're testing me. That seems like a double punishment."

"The verdict has been made," Alexander replied. "And you would do well to learn your new station in this world. Council, will you stay and act as witnesses?" Alexander asked, while the witch, Yasha, seemed to be digging through her bag for something.

One by one, each member agreed to stay and watch.

"Dominick, Samuel, Tamsin, you three are free to go. Please wait outside."

Tamsin's eyes met mine. She reached out and squeezed my arm as she was ushered out of the room. "I'm sorry," she whispered, her golden eyes bright.

"It's okay," I replied, but she was already past me. These guys were not wasting any time.

Sarah remained at my side, her hand resting on my shoulder as Yasha collected what she needed and returned to Graves and me.

"Hold out your hands," she ordered.

Warily, I obeyed. Before I could so much as wonder what she was going to do, Yasha's hand slashed out, a silver dagger making a deep cut in the fleshy part of my palm.

"Son of a bitch," I muttered, jerking my hand back instinctively.

Yasha caught my wrist before I could pull away, repeating the motion on Graves. "Now, press your hands together, palm to palm."

"I don't think that's very sanitary," I muttered.

Graves didn't even flinch at the cut, although his eyes burned like blue fire when he turned to face me.

My arm shook as I tried to resist. That's when I realized that Sarah wasn't here for comfort. She was here to ensure that I obeyed. I sighed, knowing that I was seriously outmatched.

Blood dripped down my arm in sticky rivulets as I lifted my hand. Not waiting for further instruction, Graves pressed his hand to mine, his eyes never once looking away. His unwavering gaze gave me strength. As shitty as this was, at least we were in it together.

Yasha held out a white piece of cloth, tying it around our hands as she uttered words that sounded like some combination of Yiddish and Latin. I couldn't make out any of them as she tied off the cloth and pressed her hands on either side of ours, saying clearly, "So mote it be."

There was a flash like fire, and I gasped as pain burned through my hand and up into my arm. When I could see past the pain, I noticed the cloth tying us together was now black.

"It is done," Yasha said with a small bow to Alexander.

"Test it," he said, his voice devoid of emotion.

Yasha slashed out again, slicing through Graves' forearm

before I could even blink. Fiery pain licked at my skin as if she were dragging an open flame along the exposed flesh.

"You've gotta be fucking kidding me right now," I lamented. Even though she hadn't come anywhere near me, blood dripped from the fresh wound carved into my forearm.

Graves' hand spasmed where it was pressed to mine, but he did not cry out. The only sign of his pain was the rapid pulse of a vein in his neck.

"Excellent," Alexander said. "Yasha, you may close the wounds. No need for them to bleed out in the Council room." Before he was finished speaking, the witch was already murmuring under her breath, her hand glowing softly as she healed us. Before I could inspect my freshly healed skin, Alexander added, "Perhaps this will teach both of you to think more carefully in the future. Welcome to the Brotherhood, Salem. See that you don't disappoint us again."

Brother, Where Art Thou'?

"Is there a vending machine in this place? Losing all this blood gives me the munchies."

Graves groaned. "How are you thinking about food *right now*?"

My stomach grumbled in answer, and I flashed him a satisfied smile, tucking a lock of hair behind my ear. "Cheer up. It could have been worse."

"How could this have possibly been any worse?" he asked, pushing the metal bar to open the door out of Town Hall.

"They could have just killed us on the spot. Or killed me and made you work in the mines. Speaking of mines—what was that short-looking dude that didn't talk much?"

"Suirek. He's a dwarf," Graves answered as we stepped outside. The sun was low in the sky, but we still had a few hours of daylight to kill.

"Dwarves are real too . . ." I muttered. "So, *Snow White and the Seven Dwarfs*—"

"Snow White was a real girl who took a real liking to

seven dwarves, and they to her. The whole prince thing was added in later. That part's not real."

Ugh. Well, to each their own.

My stomach rumbled again, bringing me back to my immediate need. "I don't know what your plan is, but I'm starving so—"

"The problem at hand has less to do with your stomach and more to do with your priorities. We're tied now. The blood rite doesn't expire. It doesn't end. I don't even think there's a way to break it."

"Look, I know I'm new to all this, and what happened today might have been my fault—"

"It was definitely your fault."

I pressed my lips together, glaring at him. "As I was saying before I was so rudely interrupted. Today sucked. The outcome kinda sucked. If there's no way to change it, though, harping on it isn't going to fix anything, and it sure as shit isn't going to find Shep's killer."

Graves scrubbed a hand down his face. "You know, sometimes I think about how nice it must be to be able to do that."

"Do what?" I asked, starting down the stairs and toward his car where Tamsin was leaning against the door.

"Move on. Just like that. Don't get me wrong; you're impulsive because of it, and we're in this problem to begin with because of you—but you just seem to roll with it no matter what happens."

I shrugged. "My mom died when I was young. Shep and I came here and then our dad died. Now my brother is dead. I keep going because I have to. That doesn't mean I forget, though. The reason I came back was for Shep.

Things are more complicated now, but that hasn't changed."

Graves made a noncommittal sound in the back of his throat as we approached the car.

"So," Tamsin drawled. "What's the plan?"

"Well, Salem is hungry," Graves said as he unlocked the car, and we all slid into our seats.

"What else is new?" Tamsin said, shaking her head.

Ignoring them, I immediately went for my purse. "You can come out now"—my words died in my throat when Shep's blue crocheted head didn't appear. "Motherfucker."

"What?" Graves and Tam asked at the same time.

I dumped the contents of my purse into my lap. Phone. Flashlight. Screwdriver. But no demonic stuffed animal. Groaning, I closed my eyes and leaned back against the seat. "Shep is at the Gamma Rho house. I need to go back."

"What?" Graves repeated, this time in anger. "Did you seriously bring a demon into—"

"It wasn't intentional!" I snapped back. "He snuck along in my purse, and when I dropped it, the bastard must have made a run for it. Again. I'd only just found him after he escaped the first time when you found me and then I got a little . . . uh . . . sidetracked."

Tamsin snickered, and I rolled my eyes.

"You're one to talk, succubus," I said, peering at Graves from the corner of my eye. He was holding onto the bridge of his nose like he was fighting a headache.

I could see Tamsin smirking in the rearview mirror. "Hey, I've been on Team Just Fuck Already from day one. You kids do you. Let me know if you need any—"

"And that's enough of that," Graves said, turning the

car on and twisting the knob on the radio volume all the way up.

Tamsin was cackling in the backseat as Graves drove back toward the university.

"I still can't believe you said that about me in front of my dad," Graves said after a moment.

"What? I can't hear you?" I mocked, holding a hand up to my ear.

Graves twisted the knob again and glowered at me while we idled at a red light. "You know I'm never going to live that down, right?"

I shrugged. "You didn't seem to have any problem watching them lay into me. It only seemed fair to share the spotlight with you. Since, you know, I am your *fuck buddy* as far as the entire supernatural council is concerned."

His blue eyes heated as they met mine before he slammed on the gas once more.

Mildly flustered by the memory of his lips on mine, I started rambling. "At least we don't have to use that stupid excuse anymore now. I mean, the Council basically assigned my training to you, right? So it's expected that we'll be spending time together. No more lying."

"If you think anyone is going to believe you two aren't banging every time you're alone together, you're dumber than your cottonheaded brother," Tamsin said.

"No one asked you, Tam."

She winked at me. "That's what best friends are for. Telling you the truth even when you don't want to hear it."

"Oh look, we're here," Graves said, pulling up to the Sigma Upsilon house.

Tamsin grinned at us. "You two try and get through the

rest of the night without killing each other, okay? I'll talk to you tomorrow," she added, leaning forward to press a kiss to my cheek before climbing out of the car.

We watched until she disappeared into the sorority house before Graves pulled back onto the road. Without Tamsin as a buffer, awkward silence descended between us.

"So are we going to talk about it?" I asked.

"Talk about what?"

"You know . . . the whole hallway make out thing . . ." I said nonchalantly.

Graves peered over at me, those eyes of blue fire setting my blood aflame. "I think I made my feelings toward you pretty clear." His tone of voice suggested he wanted to pick up where we left off, but the parking lot for Gamma Rho was right around the corner.

"Alrighty then." I wasn't sure what that made us exactly, but at the moment it didn't particularly matter.

Graves pulled into the parking lot and cut the engine.

I hopped out of the passenger side, leaving my purse in the car and slamming the door behind me. Graves followed after.

"Okay, so I think we should start in the hallway where I lost him," I said, flinging the back door open. We stepped inside, not alone anymore. A couple of brothers lingered in the main living area. The fridge closed from the kitchen beside us, lumberjack boy, AKA Samuel, peered over.

"Back so soon? Looking for another reaper to finish what Graves couldn't?"

While I wanted to punch him for how he treated Tamsin, I couldn't help but snort. Beside me, Graves turned icy.

"Fuck off, Sam. I wasn't the one caught getting head from a fairy two years ago in a public bathroom while her werewolf boyfriend fucked you in the ass."

Samuel turned a deep shade of red, but didn't say anything more as he turned to the kitchen counter and started making a sandwich. I let out a laugh as Graves grabbed my forearm and pulled me through the main area, not bothering with introductions as we headed straight for the stairs up to the second floor.

"How would that work with a fairy and—"

"So not the time, Salem," Graves replied. He released my wrist at the top of the stairs and turned on a dime. His pace was brisk as he walked the hallway lined with doors, going straight for the one at the very end. He grasped the handle, opening it and peering in.

Dread filled me before he even said a word.

"Not here."

I hung my head, pinching my forehead. "Fuck."

"We need to find him before another reaper does," Graves said, closing the door.

"No shit. He could be anywhere, though. This place is huge," I said as I motioned to the building. "We should split up. How about I take the top floor and—"

Graves lifted an eyebrow. "Not happening."

"What?" I asked defensively. "I'm a reaper now. I mean, I was before—but it's official now."

"Yeah, and you're looking for an excuse to snoop. I'm going to take the top floor. You go check the main floor before we start looking in rooms. If we gotta check those and we get caught, there will be hell to pay—and this time it's Dom we'll be answering to. I, for one, don't want to deal with his shit again today."

I could agree with that logic. "Fine, but what do I say if they ask why I'm here?"

Graves shrugged. "Do what you do best. Tell them the truth."

With that, he reopened the door and disappeared on the other side. It shut with an audible click. I grumbled, but like the good Salem I was, got to it.

I made my way back down the stairs with no real destination in mind. What I remembered of the layout was limited to the brief glimpses I'd caught earlier that day. At the bottom of the stairs, I turned left, heading into what looked like a game room. There was a massive flat screen television, every gaming console produced since 1972, a couple of stand-up arcade games, a ping pong—or more accurately beer pong—table, and an air hockey table. In the rest of the space, sofas, recliners, and a couple of bean bag chairs littered the floor. A few reapers were lounging around, making bets about whatever was happening on the screen. They didn't even notice me as I moved around them, eyes scanning the ground for a sign of a little blue sheep.

I wasn't sure what Shep was up to, but I couldn't imagine he'd be heading for an overly populated area. With that in mind, I stepped out of the game room and into the main entryway. Crossing that, I moved into what looked like a library. Not surprisingly, this room was empty. Rows of shelving overflowing with leather bound books and random items surrounded the space. I moved inside, eyes glazing over as I briefly inspected the titles. The center of the room was mainly taken up by a beautiful wooden table.

Peering under the table, I whispered, "Shep? You in here?"

For once I was hoping to hear his annoying little bleat, but there was nothing but silence.

"Well that's a nice view," a voice said behind me.

My head slammed into the bottom of the table before I pushed myself back into a standing position. "Uh, thanks?" I said, rubbing my head.

The guy was tall, and handsome in a preppy East Coast kind of way. He was too pretty for my taste, though, with his feathered blond hair and chocolate eyes.

"Can I help you with something?" he asked, seeming more amused than suspicious.

"I, uh, lost my stuffed animal," I said, taking Graves' advice and going with the truth.

He raised a brow my answer. "Were you here for a sleepover or something?"

I smirked. "Or something. It fell out of my purse earlier; my brother gave it to me . . . before he died. I've sort of kept it with me ever since."

Preppy's eyes filled with sympathy. "You must be Salem. I'm Dale." He held out a well-manicured hand.

I shook it. "Nice to meet you."

"Would you like some help with your search?"

"Nah, that's okay. I wouldn't want to interrupt your evening, but if you, uh, see a little blue sheep running— lying—around," I immediately corrected, hoping he didn't pick up on my slip, "could you give me a holler?"

"Sure thing." Dale gave me a little salute and turned and left the room.

I watched him leave, happy to know that not every reaper was a mega asshole when my phone gave a little chime. I jumped, having forgotten it was in my pocket.

Pulling it out, I saw that I had a text from Graves. *Is he really that lazy he couldn't just come down and get me?*

Found him.

That was it. Just two words.

"Over excited much?" I muttered, stuffing the phone back in my pocket as relief flooded me. At least one thing was going my way today. Ducking out of the library, I hurried back to the stairs, freezing at the sound of Dom's voice.

"I can't believe the Council let them off so easy," he was saying from somewhere behind me.

Shit. Even though I technically had a right to be here now, Fuckface was the last person I wanted to run into. I'd had my fill of his toxic masculinity for one day. I took the stairs two steps at a time, running down the hall and beelining for the door where I'd last seen Graves.

Flinging it open, I stepped inside and closed it as quietly as I could behind me. The locked clicked, and I let out a heavy exhale.

Gathering my wits, I looked up the dark stairway. At the very top the silver door stood out in sharp relief, despite the lack of light. I climbed the stairway as quickly and quietly as possible.

It was only just beginning to cross my mind how strange it was that Graves hadn't wanted me in here, and yet he texted me instead of coming downstairs. I shook my head, reaching for the handle made of bone. Guys were weird sometimes. Right?

I opened the door.

My heart dropped into my stomach.

No. Not fucking right. I was dead wrong.

Up in Flames

"WHAT'S GOING ON?" I ASKED, RAPIDLY TRYING TO understand the situation.

The room was large and old. While maintained like the rest of the house, this one had clearly been kept in its original state for a purpose, instead of being remodeled. With only a single dated window, antique shelves full of old books that resembled the summoning one Darla gave me, and mismatched furniture—I wasn't sure what to make of it, but I didn't really have the time.

Not with Graves' younger brother, James, standing beside the fireplace. In his hand was a wriggling blue sheep being dangled inches above the flames.

"Salem, I see you got my text," James said, flashing a phone I could only assume was Graves'. Halfway across the room, but still a good ten feet away from him, stood Graves.

"James, what are you doing with that sheep?" I asked, slowly starting for it. My heart thundered in my chest.

While the flames wouldn't destroy his soul, I would lose the only connection I had to my brother.

"Saaaaalem," my brother bleated. I ignored him for the time being.

"This one?" he asked, like it wasn't obvious. "Well, you see, I found it on my way up here to grab a book. It was very curious, a demon ending up in the house. I figured I'd take a seat and wait for the person who was concealing it to come back."

"He's mine," I said in a rush. "I dropped him when I was here earlier—"

Beside me, Graves had yet to move or speak. James seemed utterly delighted, and I didn't understand.

"Yes, my brother told me that part. When I asked him why you had a demon, he neglected to answer. Demons are dangerous, Salem. How this one ended up in your possession . . . well that's a story I'd like to hear."

I nibbled on my bottom lip.

James seemed a bit off, and that wasn't just because he was dangling Shep over a fireplace. Something just didn't seem *right* with him.

But he was Graves' brother.

"Why did you text me from Graves' phone instead of coming to find me?" I asked, deflecting instead.

"My brother wouldn't answer my questions. I thought you might. Come now, Salem. I saw you at the Bitter Bean. You aren't surprised in the slightest by this little guy moving. I know you know more than you're playing at. Why do you have a demon?"

I swallowed hard. He might be Graves' brother, but he also took his phone.

He might not be Dom, but he couldn't be trusted. That was for damn sure.

"I . . . found him," I said, trying to not look away.

"Baaaaad Saaaalem," the sheep bleated louder. If it weren't so dire, I might have been amused my brother had it in him to call me bad in a situation like this.

"Found him?" James repeated, clearly not buying it. "Where did you find him?"

"I—uh—at . . . the graveyard?" I said, answering it more like a question. Inside, I cursed myself. Stupid inability to lie.

"I don't even know you, but you're a terrible liar. So let's try this again—how'd you end up with a demon? If you don't want to tell the truth, well, I'll just have to toss him in the fire. Demons are illegal to keep, you know. It's my duty as a reaper to eliminate any I come across."

My heart was racing so fast that I felt like I could puke. The situation was so far out of my control, I wasn't sure how to even proceed. How had it escalated so quickly?

"Why are you just sitting there?" I hissed at Graves, trying to buy myself more time as I scrambled to think up an excuse.

His blue eyes shot to mine, a warning I did not remotely understand shining in them. Was he telling me to watch what I said? To stay away from his brother? I already knew we were fucked, so anything other than specifics wasn't going to help me.

James' smile grew at my question. "My big brother knows something you don't."

"Oh? What's that?" I asked, trying to keep my voice calm.

"Ah ah ah," he sing-songed, "you still haven't answered my question, Salem. Why do you have a demon?" With each word, he lowered the sheep until the flames were less than an inch away from his face.

"No! Please stop. I'll . . . I'll tell you, okay?"

"I'm waiting," James said, his hand steady once more.

"Saaaaaalem noooooooo," Shep screeched.

"It's my brother," I blurted, the words coming out in a rush. "I found a spell to summon him back. I wanted to see if I could find out who killed him, but—"

James froze, his eyes wide as he looked from me to the squirming stuffie in his hand. "Shepard Kaine, is that you?"

The sheep squirmed harder, as if in answer.

"Well . . . that's unfortunate," James said, sighing.

I watched in slow motion as he released the sheep from his pinched fingers.

Shep dropped into the fireplace as a scream tore through my throat.

There was a blur of black as Graves moved faster than my traumatized brain could track. He tackled his brother while his left arm shot out, grasping the stuffed animal by its back leg, just barely saving it from the flames.

The reapers fell to the ground in a tangle of limbs. Graves lost his hold on my brother as he hit the ground. I watched Shep somersault across the ground, only coming to a stop when he hit the wall. He let out a pitiful moan, his tiny body splayed out like a starfish.

I rushed forward, trying to dodge flying limbs as I plucked my singed brother off of the ground.

"Saaaaalem," he said, his voice weak.

"Save your energy. I'm a little busy right now," I growled, setting him on a nearby table.

A surge of pain in my hand had me spinning back

around. Graves had his brother pinned; his right arm cocked back as he prepared to slam it back into his brother's face. I could feel the impact in my knuckles as bone met bone. But the pain was fleeting.

A shimmer of something metallic caught my eye.

"Graves! Watch out!"

But it was too late. James had already jammed the knife into his brother's side.

I dropped to my knees as pain tore through my body.

James' eyes were on me as he pushed his brother's body off of him. "Well, now that's interesting."

Fucking blood rite. It hadn't even been an hour and already it was going to be the end of me.

My insides were on fire. My stomach felt like it was being torn apart. Graves fell back, hitting the floor flat on his back and trying, but struggling, to get back to his feet.

Blood poured faster from both of us.

"You two have been keeping secrets," James said, his voice eerily excited. "The blood rite hasn't been used in a very long time. Not since the dawn of our kind, when training reapers to be warriors was its most paramount. I'm curious how you two ended up bound together." James scratched his chin with a bloodied hand.

"You—piece—of shit," I gasped, struggling with my words.

James' eyebrows lifted. "Your brother's last words were more meaningful, but I must say I prefer yours." He grinned diabolically. The guy was absolutely insane. When I'd talked to him a couple weeks ago he'd been cold, but he hadn't seemed . . . crazy. But he was. Undeniably. And this whole time it was Dom I thought had killed Shep. Now, I was going to die for that mistake.

"Why?" Graves asked, trying and failing once more to get to his feet.

Fucker was killing us faster.

"Why?" James repeated, pondering the question. "I could tell you. I haven't told anyone. But then, I'd have to give a shit what you two thought. No, I think I'll let you go to the other side wondering." He walked across the rickety floors.

Greater dread filled me as I saw him lift Shep from the table.

No. My words moved to say it, but no sound came out as he walked back to the fireplace and tossed the sheep in.

My only consolation as I watched the crocheted form go up in flames was that Shep couldn't feel pain.

But me? I was still in a fuck ton of it.

I opened my mouth and inhaled as deeply as I could, and then I let out the mother of all screams.

James looked on. His watery blue eyes cold as he made no move to stop me.

"Scream all you like," he said, smiling cruelly. "This room is warded. Not a sound in or out."

The edges of my vision began to darken.

Goddamnit. No. I couldn't go. Not like this. Not when I'd only just found out who killed my brother. I couldn't let him win.

But I also couldn't stop him.

Pressing my hand to my stomach, I leaned up, willing my torso off the ground. James stood by the fire, watching me curiously. Bastard wasn't even scared. Why should he be? I had no weapon. No anything.

Still I crouched forward and pulled my feet beneath me one at a time.

I stood on shaking legs.

James clapped.

"You have balls. I like it. Too bad you fell for the wrong brother. Your face is rather pretty."

If I could have been disgusted, I would have. As it was, I barely had it in me to take that first step. Then another. And another. Until I stood before him.

"See you in hell, bitch," I said, using all my weight to throw my head forward.

I hit him square in the nose. Something crunched. He fumbled backwards, and I went with him, unable to hold my weight any longer.

Hands shoved me away and my body hit the ground hard. The pain was starting to ebb. Numbness was coming over me. The cold beginning to set in.

"I'd say you'll regret that, but you already do."

I couldn't tell where the voice was coming from.

A shoe appeared in front of my face. Stars burst behind my eyes as it all went black.

The last thing I heard was Graves' rasped breath as he laid beside me.

And then there was nothing.

Here We Go Again

WHEN I CAME TO I WAS STANDING, STARING AT the outside of a green dumpster and not up at the raftered ceiling of the creepy reaper room. I looked down, disoriented as I checked my body for a sign of the stab wound. As I'd already started to suspect, there wasn't one.

"Oh, fuck, not again," I complained.

"Salem?"

Now that, I hadn't expected.

"Graves?" I spun toward the voice, hope mingling with fear. If he was here, what did it mean? Were we both dead-dead? Or only that in-between dead like the first time I'd snuffed it? And if I was dead for real this time, did that mean I'd get to see Shep?

"What happened? How'd we get in the alley?"

I shook my head, my eyes drinking him in. Even dead he looked fucking perfect. Why did men have it so easy? Ugh. "I don't know how we got outside, but your psychotic brother definitely just killed us."

"He—" Graves started.

"Is fucking looney tunes," I finished for him.

Graves sighed. "Yeah. I don't know how to process that yet."

"I don't get it," I said. "I was so sure it was Dom. He was such an asshole. Ugh. I'm not apologizing for blaming him." I crossed my arms over my chest, peering around the backlot behind Gamma Rho.

It was dead.

Get it?

I chuckled under my breath.

"What are you laughing about now?" Graves asked, clearly less amused.

"Nothing," I said. "Just that that it's dead out here. Get it?"

He most certainly did not.

"Shouldn't there be like a white light or something?" Graves asked, looking around.

I frowned. "I'm not sure. The last time this happened Not-Morticia told me I had to go back . . ." I trailed off. "You don't think?"

Graves gave me an odd look. "Think what?"

I scratched my head, a half-formed idea taking shape in my mind. "Where the hell is a ghost when you need one?"

"You rang?" Eddie intoned, appearing out of nowhere.

"Don't do that," I hissed, although I was more startled than anything.

He blinked at me. "You asked for me, and here I am."

"Yeah, I guess I did."

Graves was looking between me and Eddie, shock etched in every line of his face. "Salem, is that . . ."

"A ghost? Can you see them now too?"

"No . . . Rumplestiltskin."

"Rumple who now? No, Graves, this is Eddie."

Graves shook his head. "No, Salem. I've seen the files. His clothes are different, but I recognize his face. That's definitely Rumplestiltskin. From the Grimm brothers' tales."

Eddie gave a little bow. "At your service."

"Huh. Okay, not really the point right now."

Graves shook his head, still looking more than a little stunned. I guess it was up to me to get to the bottom of this.

"Um, Ed—I mean, Rumpy,"—the two men grimaced at the nickname, which only ensured it was permanent—"is there somewhere we're supposed to go now?"

He looked confused. "Back into your bodies."

"Our bodies?" I looked around as if I'd perhaps missed seeing our corpses lying on the asphalt.

He pointed to the dumpster.

"Oh, you've got to be kidding me," I said, moving to lift the large black lid. Instead of budging, I went face-first into the trash can. "Ugh. Yup, there they are." Pulling myself back out of the dumpster, I turned to face Graves. "Your asshole brother tossed us out here, probably so no one would catch him. Shit murderer he is. I don't know how no one has caught his ass yet."

Graves was still staring at Rumpy like he was some kind of celebrity.

"Hey! Did you hear me? Our bodies are in there."

"So?" Graves asked, looking at me.

"So, if we want to not be ghosts for all eternity, then we need to hop back in and climb out of the dumpster so we can go kick your brother's scrawny ass." I grinned, already imagining the look on his stupid face when he saw I was still very much alive. *Surprise, motherfucker.*

"Salem, we're dead. There is no hopping back in."

"Correction, we're temporarily dead. You heard Rumpy. We just need to get our spirits back in our bodies and we're good as new."

"That's not how it works," Graves said, shaking his head.

I shrugged. "Are you really going to argue about a second—or is it third—chance at life?"

Graves rolled his eyes. "We can try it your way, but when you're wrong—"

"Then you can say I told you so and be my own personal version of Hell. Just get your ass over here."

He reluctantly walked over and peered inside. "Are you sure about this?" he asked. "Reapers only get one death, and consequently it's always blown for initiation."

"Pretty sure," I said, wrapping my arms around the metal edge of the dumpster. Using all those muscles I'd been making the past few weeks, I lifted myself up, although if I was being honest my body just sort of floated upward because I wanted it. Too bad it wouldn't work like that when I got back.

I swung my legs over the edge and landed next to our bodies.

"Come on." I moved closer to my own. "All you have to do is touch it—"

My words were drowned out the second I placed a hand on my ankle.

Everything faded for a brief moment and next thing I

knew I was staring up at the black top of the dumpster. I knew it wasn't oblivion by the smell.

"Ew," I whined, moving to sit up among all the garbage.

Something stirred next to me. I jumped, banging my head on the lid. "Ow. Motherfucker," I cursed.

"Salem?" Graves breathed; his voice soft. Confused.

"Graves!" I exclaimed. "You're alive too. I'll be damned."

"Salem, what is going on? We were dead—I saw Rumpelstiltskin—and then you touched your body and—" He spoke fast, having trouble keeping up with the absurdity of it.

I reached up and flung the top back. It hit the brick wall of Gamma Rho with a clang, but no one came running. No one jumped out of the shadows. No one was waiting for us.

It was just midnight, moonlight, and us two in the dumpster.

"Give me a leg up, will ya?" I asked, turning to him.

"How are you dealing with this so . . . easily?" he asked, leaning up. Instead of lacing his hands together as I'd expected, he grabbed me by the waist and tossed.

My feet barely cleared the edge of the dumpster before I came back down. I landed in a crouch, ankles feeling weak from the jarring impact. I stood up and didn't bother dusting myself off. There was no point. Not with blood and trash all over me. Something had leaked from one of the bags and onto my shirt that smelled awfully suspicious and made me want to gag.

Graves hauled himself out of the dumpster, landing next to me a lot more gracefully.

It might have been attractive if not for how we smelled.

"Well?" he prompted.

"Oh, yeah—well, it's like I said. I just keep going. This is how it happened last time. For a second there I thought I was dead-dead, but apparently that's not the case. It wouldn't be the first time I was wrong about how death works. Anyway, at least I get a second chance at kicking your brother in the balls and making him pay for killing us . . . and Shep." A tiny bit of sadness leaked into my voice as I thought of my brother in sheep form. The stuffie was most definitely gone, but that didn't mean he was. Not permanently. I could summon him again.

Warm fingers brushed against my forearm. I shivered.

"Hey," Graves said. "I'm sorry for not believing you when you told me that a reaper was involved. I still don't see why or how James is working with a werewolf, or how any of this came to be . . . but we'll figure it out. After a shower."

"And food," I added.

Instead of the usual ire I got at the mention of eating, a wry smile crossed his lips. He reached down and stuffed a hand in his jeans, pulling out his keys.

"Shall we?" he asked.

"Actually, I have a better plan," I said, tapping my finger against my lip before realizing what I was doing and where that finger had been. I dropped my hand back to my side. "We get my purse out of your car and take my car back to my place. As soon as your car goes missing, James will know something's up. We need to shower, and eat— and possibly eat again—before regrouping. I'm just giving you a heads-up now, your bro isn't off the hook just 'cause you're related. If it weren't for the whole being tossed in a trash can thing, I'd be half tempted to go kick his ass now."

Graves unlocked his car, and I crossed the parking lot, quickly retrieving my purse.

"It wouldn't solve anything, except pissing off the Council more and painting a bigger target on your back because I hate to break it to you, but—"

I held up a hand for him to stop talking as we started for the Sigma Upsilon house where my car was parked.

"I know you think I handle everything that happens to me super easily and that it seems like I don't have any reaction. It may look that way, but that's not exactly how it works. I'm tired. I'm cranky. I wanna beat the shit out of your brother, but I recognize I have to wait for a hot minute. So please, don't make this any worse until I get a shower and some fucking Hostess cupcakes."

"Okay," he said.

I gaped at him. "Really?" I asked, not entirely sure I had heard him correctly.

"You asked me to be quiet—"

"Never mind, go back to that quiet thing," I said, taking the back way through the bushes to avoid any unwanted attention. The sound of moans distracted me for a moment, as did the rocking back and forth of one of the cars in the parking lot.

Graves and I shared a look.

"Do you think that's—"

"Keep walking," Graves said, motioning forward. I shook my head, clearing my thoughts as I crossed the rest of the parking lot and made it to the Impala.

"Hold up," I said as he opened the door to the

passenger side. Opening the trunk, I pulled out a blanket. "Sit on this."

He raised a brow. "I'm not sure a lone blanket is going to do much."

"It's one less seat that will have to be detailed. Just use it."

Graves chuckled as he unfolded the blanket and sat on it. "I didn't take you for someone who'd get prissy about the interior of her car."

Starting the engine, I gave him an incredulous look. "What's that supposed to mean?"

He shrugged. "I dunno, you just—"

"It isn't just any car, okay? It's the one you worked on with my twin, and right now it's pretty much the last thing of his in my life, so just—"

Graves rested his hand on my knee, cutting off the flood of words. "It's okay, I get it. I'm sorry if I pushed the wrong button."

"As opposed to all the other times?"

"God, you make it impossible to say nice things to you," he said, throwing his head against the headrest.

I laughed. "Shep used to say the same thing."

Grave tilted his head my way, his lips lifting in a hint of a smile. "Want to know a secret?"

"Haven't you had enough of those already?"

"I think you'll like this one."

"Alright, shoot," I said, gunning the engine as I got out of the town and into the less populated area.

"Shep used to tell me the same thing."

I snickered, not at all surprised that my brother would find Graves just as stubborn and pigheaded as me. It's why we butted heads so easily, and why we both seemed to enjoy annoying the shit out of each other so much.

Maybe Tam was right, and it was just our weird version of foreplay.

"Hey, Salem?"

"Hmm?" I replied, his question pulling me out of my musings.

"Is Esme home?"

"Oh shit," I cursed, wondering how the hell I was going to explain our current state to her. Then I remembered who we were talking about. Esme was the queen of weird. I just had to think of some hobby that involved us being in the trash. "Do you think she'd believe that we were dumpster diving for like recycling or something?"

Graves gave me a look. "Maybe you should leave the excuses to me."

"You're probably right," I agreed, barely slowing down as I made a left turn onto Mansion Lane.

A few minutes later, I slowed as I turned up the drive and parked the car. The porch lights were out, which meant Esme was either asleep or not at home. Maybe we wouldn't need that excuse after all.

"I'm going to keep the lights off just in case she's sleeping. Try not to knock anything over," I whispered as I started to unlock the door.

"Uh, Salem. I think you're forgetting that I've seen you trying to be sneaky. Trust me, I'm not the one you need to worry about."

I stuck my tongue out at him over my shoulder as I pushed the door open and let us inside. We weren't completely silent, but almost, especially with our hearing. I shut the door behind us and made it two steps before some-thing went whizzing past my right side.

A loud *thunk* made me jump.

I scrambled to flip the light on.

Nailed in the wooden frame only two inches above Graves' head was an arrow.

What the fu—

"Oh, it's you," came my aunt's voice. I followed the path from the arrow all the way across the room to where my aunt stood with a crossbow. My mouth fell open, then closed as I tried to find words.

"Esme," I said in shocked breath. "What the fuck are you doing?" It seemed my words came back, and judging by my aunt's face, she wasn't thrilled with the ones I chose. "You nearly shot him in the head with a crossbow!"

"I was practicing," she answered defensively. Ten feet to my side a heavy blanket was draped over the staircase and a red bullseye was spray painted on it. Bolts stuck in the fabric and the paint dripped onto the hardwood floors.

"At midnight?" I asked.

"It's not my fault you two startled me *at night* trying to sneak in the house like you're up to no good. Come now, Salem, you remember that talk we had about *me time*. I've got a great brand I can recommend that'll surely do better than this one." She motioned with her elbow and sniffed once. "Any guy sneaking into your house and smelling like trash ain't worth the quick scratch."

My face flamed red. "We are *not* having this talk right now," I said, grabbing Graves' wrist and stepping further into the room. I tried to keep myself between him and her at all times. "Graves and I are just friends. We're going to . . .

do a thing. Please, can you refrain from practicing with a crossbow in the house next time?" I looked from her to the makeshift shooting range she'd made of the entryway.

"Mmm," was the only response I got as we started down the hall. "Make sure to use condoms," she called after us. "I'm not sure how smart this one is, and I don't need dumb grandkids."

If my face weren't already on fire, it would be now. I didn't grace her insults with a response as I opened my bedroom door and motioned for Graves to go in.

"Okay," he said slowly. "Your aunt is officially nuts."

"Sorry?" I offered half-heartedly, closing the door behind us. "She's usually not this bad. She's gone off the deep end since Shep died and is handling his passing in her own weird way."

"That's putting it mildly," Graves said under his breath before turning his attention to my room. My bed wasn't made. My shoes had been haphazardly tossed in my closet and clothes were spilling out of the door. At least I didn't have any dirty laundry laying around.

I opened my bathroom door and pulled a stack of towels out, setting them on the counter.

"You cool showering in Shep's room? You can take whatever you need to wear. I'll shower here, then order us some pizza since Esme is being weird."

"You sure?" he asked hesitantly.

"Yeah, it's right across the hall. I wish I could lie and say I'm doing it to be nice, but really I don't want to wait to shower and you're also disgusting." Graves gave me that look most people gave me when they couldn't believe what came out of my mouth. Not saying anything, he grabbed a towel from my stack and headed toward the door, shaking his head while he did so.

I closed the bathroom door and stripped my nasty clothes from my skin. Taking my first real look in the mirror, I wasn't sure how my aunt didn't ask more questions. My hair was a pink bird's nest with strands sticking out in every direction. Dark circles lined my bloodshot eyes. Red smudged my neck and lower. Fortunately, most of the blood not being near my face probably helped. That and the all black clothes I'd been wearing.

I took one look at them and wrinkled my nose, tossing them into the trash can before flipping the shower on as hot as it could go. As soon as steam started to fog the glass walls, I stepped inside. My skin went from chilled to burning as the two water jets did most of the work. I washed and scrubbed every part of me, not giving two shits that most of the hair dye was bleeding into the water along with the blood and gunk from earlier.

When my skin was sufficiently pink and my stomach grumbling enough to pull me away from the shower, I flipped the lever off and stepped out. Water dripped from my skin as I wrapped myself in one of the fluffy towels and used a second one for my hair.

I opened my bedroom door to see Graves sitting on my bed. He lifted his face, and our eyes met. If my cheeks weren't already red from the water, they would have been then.

"What?" I said.

His eyes traveled my form before returning to my face. "Nothing."

The word *liar* was on the tip of my tongue, but my

stomach gurgled again, and reality came back. I retreated to my walk-in closet, closing the door behind me as I dressed in a pair of sweatpants and a T-shirt. Once dressed, I flipped my head a few times, letting my shaggy bob air-dry as I stepped back into my room.

Graves opened his mouth to speak. I held up a finger as I picked up my phone. "First step, pizza. Then you can talk."

"At least no one will ever doubt your priorities."

"Preferences?" I asked as I dialed the pizza place by memory.

"I'm not even surprised you have their number memorized."

"Last chance," I said, flipping him off as the line rang.

"Anything with meat," he answered.

I ordered us two large pizzas, mostly ignoring his raised eyebrows when I added on an order of breadsticks, hot wings, and chocolate lava cake. I'd just died. Again. I was going to eat whatever I wanted, and I was starting with the cake.

Hanging up the phone, I settled next to him on the bed. "Alright, now you may speak and say all of the dire things."

Graves studied me, an odd expression crossing his face. "You know, before tonight, I thought I knew pretty much everything there was to know about the supernatural world."

"That's funny. Before tonight I already knew I didn't have a clue about any of it."

Graves grinned at me. "I should have remembered the cardinal rule. It can always get worse."

"Yeah, no kidding. At least we seem to be immune to dying, or whatever," I said, playing with my sweatpants.

"Salem," he said, his voice tentative, "that's not a thing. Reapers only come back once. Whatever you are . . . I don't think you're a reaper."

"Really, because a few days ago you were certain I was." My gaze held onto his, but he extended a hand, begging me with his eyes to let him finish.

"I've been on the fence for a while. I mean, female thing aside, you seem to be able to do stuff that no other reapers can do, and not much of what they can. The seeing and talking to ghosts for one, your crazy speed, and now this."

I don't know why it felt harder to accept this possibility than everything else that had happened since coming home. I'd died and come back. Been told I was a reaper, and that my dad and twin were too . . . I felt like it fit. Like there was a piece of them I didn't have before but maybe I would now. It had made an odd sort of sense. But now I was different. Other. Unknown.

"How is that even possible?" I finally asked.

"I don't know," he admitted softly. "But we're going to find out."

"How? You just said you don't have a clue what I am."

"So? That doesn't mean someone else won't. I'm sure Darla probably knows something she didn't tell us last time."

"Okay . . . but what about you? You came back too."

"I think the blood rite had something to do with it."

"So, you can't die because I can't?" I asked, thinking through the implications of that.

Graves scratched the back of his neck. "I think so? I'm

guessing here. This is all way out of my comfort zone. A few days ago—hell, a couple hours ago—I would have told you this entire conversation was impossible, but now that I'm living it..." he trailed off and shrugged.

I flopped back on my bed and stared up at the ceiling. "I'm going to need an entire truckload of Hostess cupcakes to deal with this."

Graves waved one of the plastic wrapped treats above my eyes. "It's not a truckload, but how about one to hold you over till the pizza gets here?"

I sat up. "Where did you get that? Don't tell me it was in your pocket when we were in the dumpster."

Graves laughed and shook his head. "No. I've been keeping a stash in the car since I know how impossible you get when you're hungry. I snagged it when you grabbed your purse. Just in case."

I was oddly touched by the thoughtfulness of it. Even if he did sound like a bit of an asshole when he said it. Ripping off the plastic wrap, I took a giant bite of sugary sweetness.

"You know, Graves, there's worse things than being what I am—whatever that is. At least if we can't die, this bullshit punishment doesn't really mean anything."

"Well, there is that."

"We still gotta deal with your brother, though," I said around a mouthful of chocolate cupcake.

Graves sighed. "For once, I think we're on the same page. Pizza first. The other shit can wait."

Despite how shitty and yet not shitty our situation was, I smiled.

Because this wasn't the end for us.

It was the beginning.

To be continued . . .

Salem's story continues in:

Stalking Reapers and Other Failed Dates

Text "Books" to (844) 506-1510
To stay up to date on future releases and sales!

If you loved this book and want to connect more with Kel and her other readers, please join her Facebook Readers Group at https://www.facebook.com/groups/ thecrowsnestreadersguild for more shenanigans!

Acknowledgments

We would like to thank the Academy for this . . . oh wait, wrong speech. First and foremost, thank you so much for taking a chance on Salem and her always-sexy-sometimes-annoying reaper. She is so much fun to write, and we laughed more writing this story than any other. Seriously, scythe text anyone?

We knew this series was going to be something special as soon as we started talking about Salem and her demon stuffie, but neither of us had any clue just how much fun it was going to be bringing it to life. We can't wait for you to see what else is in store for Baaaaaaad Salem.

To all our alpha readers, thank you for the love and support. Your encouragement helped bring this story to life.

A – Special thanks to you. This story wouldn't be what it is today without you.

About Kel Carpenter

Kel Carpenter is a master of werdz. When she's not reading or writing, she's traveling the world, lovingly pestering her co-author, and spending time with her family. She is always on the search for good tacos and the best pizza. She resides in Maryland and desperately tries to avoid the traffic.

Join Kel's Readers Group!

www.ingramcontent.com/pod-product-compliance
Lightning Source LLC
Chambersburg PA
CBHW030823210726

48290CB00002B/726